Poetry Explorers

British Isles

Edited by Vivien Linton

First published in Great Britain in 2009 by

Remus House
Coltsfoot Drive
Peterborough
PE2 9JX
Telephone: 01733 890066
Website: www.youngwriters.co.uk

All Rights Reserved
Book Design by Spencer Hart
Illustrations by Ali Smith
© Copyright Contributors 2009
SB ISBN 978-1-84924-317-9

Foreword

At Young Writers our defining aim is to promote an enjoyment of reading and writing amongst children and young adults. By giving aspiring poets the opportunity to see their work in print, their love of the written word as well as confidence in their own abilities has the chance to blossom.

Our latest competition Poetry Explorers was designed to introduce primary school children to the wonders of creative expression. They were given free reign to write on any theme and in any style, thus encouraging them to use and explore a variety of different poetic forms.

We are proud to present the resulting collection of regional anthologies which are an excellent showcase of young writing talent. With such a diverse range of entries received, the selection process was difficult yet very rewarding. From comical rhymes to poignant verses, there is plenty to entertain and inspire within these pages. We hope you agree that this collection bursting with imagination is one to treasure.

Contents

Ballasalla Primary School, Malew, Isle of Man

Mila Clague (10) 1
Anna Clarke-Smith (10) 3
Dylan Livingston-Chambers (10) 3
Conrad Fletcher (10) 4
Kieran Thompson (10) 5
Paul Knighton (10) 6
George Powell (10) 7
Susannah McGrath (10) 8
Nathan Hill (10) 9
Matthew Roosen (10) 10
Zach Taylor (10) 11
Conor Garrett (10) 12
Ben Cregeen (10) 12
Rebecca Storrie (10) 13
Cameron Rhys Staniford (10) 13
Jaynie Skillicorn (10) 14
Leah Turner (10) 14

Bowmore Primary School, Bowmore, Isle of Islay

Scott MacCalman (11) 15
Andrew MacNeill (10) 15
Hannah Louise Gillies (10) 16
Joseph Hughes (10) 17
Natalie Dunn (10) 18
Dylan Cummings (10) 19

Buchan School, Castletown, Isle of Man

Louis Scott (8) 19
Sami Benbatoul (11) 20
Gemma Tipper (8) 21
Jennifer Catherine Martin (8) 22
Alexander Vanderplank (8) 22

Castel Primary School, Castel, Guernsey

Joshua Dowinton (10) 23
James Christian (9) 24
Robyn Munro (9) 25
Dylan James (9) 26
Oliver Toussaint (9) 27
Thomas Upson (8) 28
Sophie Le Feuvre (9) 29
Ruby Davison (8) 30
Erin Harris (7) 30
Rebecca Cox (10) 31
Anna Renouf (9) 31

Murray's Road School, Douglas, Isle of Man

Joseph Cowin (10) 32
Connor Shakespeare (9) 33
Dylan Luke Fearon (9) 33
Hannah Charlotte Cuthbert (9) 34
Sarah-Jane Catherine Bell (10) 35
James Crook (9) 35
Yasmin Bell (9) 36
Gabriella Lulu Swan May Hay (9) 36
Robert James Blenkinsop (10) 37
Jacob Brand (9) 37
Gareth Lee Chilcott (9) 38
Jorja Marie Christian (10) 38
Lucy Banks (10) 39
Jack Goodwin (10) 39
Rachel Elizabath Crook (9) 40
Luke Bateman (10) 40
Lainna Garcia (8) 41
Lisa Cross (10) 41
Megan Birch (9) 42
Anton Ivshin (10) 42

Karl Andrew Callister (10) 43
Hannah Joan Sayle (10) 43

Notre Dame Du Rosaire Primary School, St Peter Port, Guernsey

Ben Holland (9) 44
Anasofia Ray (8) 44
Ellie Holland (10) 45
Esmee Guilbert-Robinson (8) 46
Molly Paul (8) 47
Daniel Ray (10) 48
Olivia Le Friec (9) 49
Christina Allen (9) 49
Tove Barnes (10) 50
Matilda Ayres (9) 51
Nicole Upton (10) 52
Hannelore Williams-Reid (8) 53
Elizabeth Correia (7) 54

SS Mary & St Michael RC Primary School, St Sampsons, Guernsey

Daniel Le Cheminant (10) 54
Joshua Ozanne 55
Aidan Brookes (10) 55
Nathan Austin (10) 56
Aaron Jordan Coulson (11) 56
Zeke Boyce (10) 57
Jordan Redwood (10) 57
Liam John Concannon (10) 58

St John's School, St John, Jersey

Kelly Dixon (10) 58
Dylan Hopwood (11) 59
Matthew Allo (11) 59
Dana Stamps (11) 60
Kira Jayne Mitchell (10) 60
Cameron Queree (10) 61
Remy Hidrio (10) 61
Tamsin D'Orleans (10) 62

St Martin's Primary School, St Martin, Jersey

Joel Fallon (8) 62
Jack Evans (8) 63
Alice Mollet (10) 64
Dylan Buesnel (11) 65
Maya Walton (8) 66
Harrison Lee Carlyon (8) 66
Skye Fox (7) 67
Rebecca Renouard (8) 67
Lucy May Hilton (7) 68
Joel Lucas-Villar (8) 68
Amy Claxton (8) 69
Chantal Le Rossignol (7) 69
Sophie Venton (8) 70
Leanne Carroll (8) 70
Lilly Simon Heslam (7) 71
Brody Boleat (8) 71
Patrick Claxton (7) 72
Shauna Danvill (9) 72
Tegan Jade Parker (7) 73
Cleo Leather (7) 73
Flora Leather (7) 74
Deacon Wilson (7) 74
Daniella Le Beurrier (7) 75
Leonel Camacho (8) 75
Lily-Mae Fry (7) 76
Katie Marett (8) 76
Callum Du Heaume (7) 77
Calvin Carroll (10) 77
Charlie Lucas (7) 77
Charis Renouf (11) 78
Molly Bettencourt (7) 78
Max Roberts (7) 78
Emily Le Gallais (7) 79
George Cousins (8) 79
Sienna Denny Mallen (11) 79
Ross Lawless (7) 80
Mark Marett (11) 80
Lucy Le Gallais (11) 80
Courtney Jane Carrel (11) 81
Joshua Michael Le Gallais (7) 81

Brandon Le Rossignol (8) 81

St Mary's RC Primary School, Douglas, Isle of Man

Orla McMullan (11) 82

St Michael's School, St Saviour, Jersey

Georgina Bourne (11) 83
Angus Drummond (9) 84
Tate Spurling (9) 85
Emma Banks (11) 86
Emilie Lindsay (11) 87
Jemima O'Connell (10) 88
Hollie Hemaya (9) 89
James Unwin (10) 90
Georgia Clews (11) 91
Elizabeth Baker (9) 91
Benedict Jones (10) 92

St Saviour's School, St Saviour, Jersey

Christopher Milon (8) 92
Cerys Griffiths (9) & Alana Ricou (9) 93
Tianne Guillaume & Lara Peters (8) 94
Ellie Carré (8) 95
Tillie Jones (8) 96

Scoill Phurt le Moirrey, Port St Mary, Isle of Man

Christopher Henthorn (6) 96
Charlie Davidson (11) 97
Christian Lockerby (8) 97
Mark Copley (9) 98
Harvey Shimmin (9) 98

Victoria College Preparatory School, St Helier, Jersey

Sam Philpot (10) 98
Alexander Clarke (11) 99
William Speck (11) 100

Joshua Le Cornu (11) 101
Ruben Le Sueur (10) 102
Max Le Feuvre (10) 103
Martin Fernando (11) 104
Philip Beaugie (11) 105
James Bowden (10) 106
Marcus de la Haye (11) 107
Alec Gibb (8) 108
Finlay Clayton (10) 109
James Russ (11) 110
Brandon Brawley (10) 111
Harry Jones (10) 112
Cameron Winch (10) 113
Guy Pim (10) 114
Alexander Hodnett (11) 114
Alexander Howell-Jackson (11) 115
Charlie Wilding (11) 115
Alexander Tucker (11) 116
Joseph Barette (11) 116
Ben Reid (11) 117
Rory Coughlan (11) 117
Daniel Ho (11) 118
Max Rimmer (11) 119
Ryan Lowe (11) 120
Reuben Gower (10) 121
Bradley Rose (11) 122
James Le Breton (10) 123
Sam King (11) 123
Max Young (10) 124
Emerson Colback (11) 125
Reuben Taylor (11) 126
Callum Harrison (11) 127
Robert Duckett (10) 128
Max Roantree (10) 128
James Jeune (11) 129
Nicholas Darwin (10) 129
William Giles (10) 130
Reuben Joseph Falle (11) 130
Massimo Furness (10) 131
George Donaldson (10) 131
Elliot Powell (11) 132
Freddie Stein (10) 132
Maximilian Hornby (10) 133

Ryan Cummins (10)	133
Charlie Gicquel (11)	134
Garth Jackson (11)	134
Morgan James (10)	135
Max Jouault (10)	136
Isaac Le Breton (10)	136
Michael Day (10)	137
Ben Timms (10)	137
Daniel McCarthy (11)	138
Reid O'Neill (10)	139
Nathan de la Haye (10)	140
Solomon Warner (11)	141
Jacob Hill (9)	142
Euan Spencer (10)	143
Jamie Smith (10)	144
Max Shepherd (10)	144
Dylan Kempster-Smyth (10)	145

The Poems

My Dog Beau

I went to the park
With my dog Beau

To play a game
Again and again

He runs like the wind
And spins and spins

It starts to snow
It flows and flows

Silently
Silently
Silently

When I came back home
With my dog Beau

I could hear the kettle boiling
Sizzling, crackling in the wind
Like a cricket in the grass

My brother chatting
Like a jack-in-the-box

My sister running in the garden
Like a cheetah in the wild

And my mother singing
Like a beautiful bird

So my dog and me
Really do love each other

Slowly
Slowly
Slowly

All snug in bed
Where I will rest my sleepy head
With my dog Beau.

Mila Clague (10)
Ballasalla Primary School, Malew, Isle of Man

My Dog, Maxie

Out at the park
Where the children play

My dog and me
Have lots of fun

She goes up to people
And sniffs and sniffs

And I, Anna, walk on
The coal-black path

She runs like a cheetah
Flowing like the wind

Quickly
Quickly
Quickly

Then when we get home
To sit down and rest

I give Maxie her food
And water to have

I close the back gate
As she pushes past

My mum in the kitchen
Making my lunch

My dad on the laptop
Doing his work

And my sister
Playing with her toys

I sit on the sofa
And have a drink
And now we are home
To sit down and rest

Quietly
Quietly
Quietly.

Anna Clarke-Smith (10)
Ballasalla Primary School, Malew, Isle of Man

Fast Car

An Aston Martin
DBS9

Has a
Top speed

Of 190mph
On a motorway.

You can drive
From England to France.

The Peel
Was made

In the Isle of Man
The top speed

Is 37mph!

Dylan Livingston-Chambers (10)
Ballasalla Primary School, Malew, Isle of Man

The Snow Cat

She chases the wind
Like a husky

Outside in the
Cold, white snow

She chases her sister
Like a buffalo

Around the white
Snowy field

She jumps at the window
Like a grasshopper

Let me in!
Let me in!
Let me in!

My mum gets up
And opens the window

Very smoothly
Like nothing is there

She sits
By the big fireplace

Snug as a bug
In a rug

She falls asleep
Like a good cat

Let her be
Let her be
Let her be!

Conrad Fletcher (10)
Ballasalla Primary School, Malew, Isle of Man

Chess

Checkmate against you
Is like being beaten up in the battlefield

When the queen attacks you
It becomes a leech swimming

At its prey as fast as
Lightning to Earth

When a pawn hits your row eight
It becomes a shape-shifter

Turning into anything
That has been

Taken
Taken
Taken by you

When you are winning, you are
The best army attacking the opponent

And you are defending
Your kingdom very easily

Your queen is attacking
The opponent king, check, you say

They move a piece, no use
You advance your rook

Checkmate
Checkmate
Checkmate!

Kieran Thompson (10)
Ballasalla Primary School, Malew, Isle of Man

Here In Moscow

Here in Moscow,
Champions League Final.

Man U and Chelsea,
Were battling it out in a match.

Memorable moment,
All English final for the first time ever.

The game starts, captains shake hands,
Scolari and Sir Alex, rivals from the Premiership.

That ball whipped in by Brown,
Is like a bird flying firmly in the air.

Ronaldo flies through the air
To meet the ball . . . *goal!*

He literally beats Carvalho by miles,
Like a parachuter in the air.

Half-time, like a couple of nano seconds away,
Lampard has just shot a bird with that goal.

Extra time hits, so does Drogba,
With that dreaded slap, *red card!*

All equal in this penalty shoot-out!

Terry scores, they win, but miss,
Anelka misses, United win the house, Van der Sar saves!

Paul Knighton (10)
Ballasalla Primary School, Malew, Isle of Man

Lola And Jaffa

Lola is my dog from England
When Lola came home

She liked my face
We played with her toys

She was so tired
She fell asleep

When she was asleep
She was snoring like my dad

Snoring
Snoring
Snoring

My cat, called Jaffa, was watching
Lola sleeping and snoring

With her green eyes
I came and picked her up

She was feather in my arms
I put her next to Lola

And she went to sleep

Sleep
Sleep
Sleep.

George Powell (10)
Ballasalla Primary School, Malew, Isle of Man

My Dog, Casper

As he went outside into the dark
He looked around

His paws
Were cold as ice

He ran around
As fast as he could

Next, he spotted a ball
And lay down and played

And played
And played

He got out of the cold
And into the light

He went and got a pair of shoes
And chewed them

As the food was sitting there
He got more anxious

And he went to his food
And ate

And ate
And ate!

Susannah McGrath (10)
Ballasalla Primary School, Malew, Isle of Man

My Cornet

Out of the case
The cornet is ice

And a scale to warm up
Like a singer warming up their voice

Out of the case
The cornet plays a bird-like song

During the song
The valves stick like glue

Out of the case
Comes the oil

It is the ocean
And the sky

It is slathered on
Shiny, silver valves

The song stops
The silence comes

Before it is put back into its case
It is emptied of all the water

In the case
Is where everything goes.

Nathan Hill (10)
Ballasalla Primary School, Malew, Isle of Man

The Night And Light

The night
Is spooky,

The night
Is dark,

It's no place
To

Play when
Midnight falls.

Light, on the
Other hand, is

Much more
Welcoming,

As bright
As the sun,

But if you
Look at it for

Too long, you
Might just

Hurt your eyes.

Matthew Roosen (10)
Ballasalla Primary School, Malew, Isle of Man

The Flower And The Thorn Bush

In a field a beautiful flower stood
And this was the most beautiful flower ever.

Its petals as bright as the sun
Its leaves as green as the grass.

And there it stood
All day long

Day long
Day long
Day long

In the coal-black forest
There was a thorn bush.

All prickles and spiky
Prickling anything

That came near
So when you see a thorn bush

Run away
Run away
Run away!

Zach Taylor (10)
Ballasalla Primary School, Malew, Isle of Man

My Dog Coco

My dog Coco,
Every morning he brings me his toys.

They squeak
Like a dead duck

In the afternoon
He growls like a wolf

Meaning, 'I'm hungry'
When I go to give him food

He runs as fast as a cheetah
When he's had his food

I play with him
When I pick him up with his toys
He looks like a flying bird!

Conor Garrett (10)
Ballasalla Primary School, Malew, Isle of Man

My Pet, Fluffy

Fluffy is the quietest hamster
In the world

He scurries round the house
All the time

And he is as fast
As a cheetah!

Ben Cregeen (10)
Ballasalla Primary School, Malew, Isle of Man

My Dog, Tag

In the garden, my dog runs around mad
And tries to jump on the trampoline

His black, shiny coat
Shines brightly in the sun

At night, he will come
Inside the house and want food

After he has had his dinner
He will go into his bed

To lie down
With his fluffy bear.

Rebecca Storrie (10)
Ballasalla Primary School, Malew, Isle of Man

Buster, My Mouse

Buster is the cutest mouse
In the world.

When he runs, he will run as fast
As bees' wings.

He also has a ball and when he's
In it, he will go half the speed.

If he gets out of his cage
Catch him
Catch him
Catch him!

Cameron Rhys Staniford (10)
Ballasalla Primary School, Malew, Isle of Man

My Hamster, Buster

My hamster, Buster, scurries around in a rush
Looking for food and bedding
When he finds his food and bedding
He runs into his bed and settles down and eats
When he has had a sleep
He comes out for a play
I let him out and put him in his ball that he runs around in
Then I put him in his cage
And he gets more food and drink
Then goes back to sleep
That's all about my hamster, Buster.

Jaynie Skillicorn (10)
Ballasalla Primary School, Malew, Isle of Man

My Pony

My pony gallops
Around the field

He slips, he nearly falls
Through the floor

I take him out
Of the field

Then I put him in his stable
He runs for the hay.

Leah Turner (10)
Ballasalla Primary School, Malew, Isle of Man

Anti-Litter

This is a poem all about litter,
Birds try to eat it, but it tastes quite bitter.
All the cans we leave on the ground,
Dogs poke their heads in, then can't see around.
Fishermen leave their guts in a mess,
When animals die of it, they will confess.
The wrapper we leave blowing in the street,
It soon attracts rats, with their claw-like feet.
Plastic bags that float in the sea,
Soon kill a whale, though you won't see.
Metal and glass, waiting on the beach,
Waiting for a child to step on them and screech.
Where should we put the paper and tins?
We all know we should put them in the bins!

Scott MacCalman (11)
Bowmore Primary School, Bowmore, Isle of Islay

Anti-Litter Poem

My poem is about anti-litter,
It makes me quite bitter.
Put that crisp packet in your jacket,
Don't leave it on the street.
Put that tin in the bin,
Don't leave it on the street.
Don't drop plastic, it's not fantastic,
Don't leave it on the street.
Don't drop a nappy, it doesn't make me happy,
Don't leave them rotting on the street.

Andrew MacNeill (10)
Bowmore Primary School, Bowmore, Isle of Islay

My Anti-Litter Poem

My poem is about anti-litter,
Seeing someone drop it, makes me feel bitter.
Sweetie wrappers blowing in my street,
Attracting rats with their dirty feet.
Tin cans ready to trap,
Little birds whose life will sap.
Without our plastic,
Our street would look fantastic.
All that glass on the street,
It hurts little dogs' feet.
Card on the ground,
Just waiting to be found.
Without litter on our streets,
Our world would look very neat!

Hannah Louise Gillies (10)
Bowmore Primary School, Bowmore, Isle of Islay

Anti-Litter

My poem is about anti-litter,
It makes me feel rather bitter.
Sweet wrappers on the street,
It doesn't look very neat.
Glass is getting dropped on the ground,
We get cut if it isn't found.
Cans sitting everywhere on the grass,
They get very rusty, but at least it doesn't turn into brass.
Plastic bottles lying about the floor,
Some people get them hidden behind the door.
Cigarettes are everywhere, it looks really bad,
It starts to make me really mad.
Don't drop litter on the ground,
You never know what could come around.

Joseph Hughes (10)
Bowmore Primary School, Bowmore, Isle of Islay

Anti-Litter Poem

My poem is about anti-litter
All the streets look rather bitter
Sitting in the street
With glass at my feet
Cans getting dropped all over the ground
No doubt a rat is going to be found
Plastic everywhere, on the grass
I tell you, don't go in the grass very fast
Thinking about all the animals in the sea
I'll make sure it wasn't me
Standing at the petrol station, petrol dripping
Hoping a dog doesn't start sipping
Don't throw the tin
Put it in the bin!

Natalie Dunn (10)

Bowmore Primary School, Bowmore, Isle of Islay

Anti-Litter Poem

My poem is about anti-litter,
When I see it, it makes me bitter,
When it attracts rats,
I would hit them with baseball bats,
When the cans catch birds,
I am speechless for words,
When the seals go out for meals,
They get caught by dirty dealers,
When a person leaves a nappy,
It makes everyone not happy,
When you drop litter,
It makes me bitter!

Dylan Cummings (10)
Bowmore Primary School, Bowmore, Isle of Islay

My Naughty Sister

My sister is naughty - she is such a whiney girl,
She always wants pearls,
She once threw me down the stairs!
So I usually call her a pear!
She is such a bully
And she talks to her friends horridly.
How her friends hate her - they think she's a moody grouch,
'I hate her!' says Jill, 'So do I,' says Bill.
'How she's always pretending to be ill,'
Complains Sam every Sunday
And she's always saying, 'Stop it!' and *'Nah-nah, ne, nah-nah!'*
Now that's my sister.

Louis Scott (8)
Buchan School, Castletown, Isle of Man

War

The war is terrible
That is true,
Hear the tale of my friend
His name was Hugh.

The first day he was
All excited inside,
For honour was yours
If ever you died.

But reality soon set in
That trenches were not playgrounds
And it certainly didn't tickle
If you were shot by a gun with five rounds.

Alas, he couldn't last too long
And that was soon true,
He was shot by a German
And that was the end of poor, poor Hugh.

Back in London, his children
Lovely little Janet and Fred,
Were playing little soldiers
Not knowing that Daddy was dead.

'Mummy! Mummy!'
Freddie and Janet would cry,
'Soon we will join the war
And we will never die.'

Let that be a lesson
So keep your children indoors,
Unless you want them killed
In those terrible, terrible wars.

Sami Benbatoul (11)
Buchan School, Castletown, Isle of Man

Food

Sausages fat,
Sausages thin,
Sausages go with anything!

Chicken in pie,
Chicken in stew,
Chicken, peas and sweetcorn too!

Duck in pancakes,
Rolled up tight,
My favourite almost any night!

Yorkshire pudding,
Golden brown,
Always removes a grumpy frown!

Sweets with sugar,
Sweets of pink,
With a lovely fizzy drink!

Portions big,
Portions small,
I love food, I love it all!

(Except *mustard!*)

Gemma Tipper (8)
Buchan School, Castletown, Isle of Man

What Happened?

What happened to the place where the children played,
The birds sang and the flowers grew?
What happened to the place where the grass was green,
The church bells rang and adventure lay?
What happened to the place where the lake was blue,
Fish all swam and the sun shone?
We want to get back there,
We must find a way,
I don't know, maybe we'll get there some day.

Jennifer Catherine Martin (8)
Buchan School, Castletown, Isle of Man

Dragon

D aring beast soaring through the air
R oaring and guarding the lonesome damsel in distress
A s hard as rock, a body of scales, only a spear shall pierce its skin
G igantic monster with arms of steel
O ver mountains it flies, never stopping to rest
N ever, ever make a dragon angry, for you shall get scorched!

Alexander Vanderplank (8)
Buchan School, Castletown, Isle of Man

The Magic Box

(Based on 'Magic Box' by Kit Wright)

I will put in the box . . .

A parrot pecking on a pineapple sundae
A menacing monkey mumbling madly
A surfing shark stupidly singing.

I will put in the box . . .

A red sky and a blue sun
A tree that can grow money
A flying fish and a swimming bird.

I will put in the box . .

The sound of my family scrunched in tin foil
The first sight of my dog
A perfectly polished PlayStation.

My box is fashioned from . . .

The sides of my box are made from silver
And the front is made from gold
The sunlight bounces off of it
With whispers in the corners
The hinges are made from my dog's nails.

I will go surfing in my box
And I will watch my past.

Joshua Downinton (10)
Castel Primary School, Castel, Guernsey

The Magic Box

(Based on 'Magic Box' by Kit Wright)

I will put in the box . . .

A whopping big whale winning the wrestling championship
An amazing Amazonian attacking an animal
And a pink parrot playing ping-pong on a Persian piranha.

I will put in the box . . .

A red sky and a blue sun
A gleaming tooth with a golden point
A flying hedgehog and a prickly swallow.

I will put in the box . . .

A woeful war game on the Wii
A green snowball made from fire
And a fire-breathing cat made from gold.

My box is fashioned from
Glass, gold and fire
The lid is polished so it reflects the light
Into prisms of multicoloured light
The hinges are made from emeralds that sparkle in the firelight.

I will play in my box
In everlasting happiness
For the world never ends.

James Christian (9)
Castel Primary School, Castel, Guernsey

The Magic Box
(Based on 'Magic Box' by Kit Wright)

I will put in my box . . .

A humungous hippo hopping hungrily
A cheeky chimp chomping chocolate
A dizzy dice doing duties.

I will put in my box . . .

The bluest sand simmering in the sun
The scariest mouth scowling stupidly
A screaming teacher playing with Barbies.

I will put in my box . . .
The wet clouds hardening up
A red emerald shining rapidly
A green ruby with sparkling eyes.

My box is fashioned from
Ice-cold rings and simmering fire
Its lid is a full star, with X marks the spot
The hinges are made from bombs set alight!

I will sing in my box and dance on the breeze
I will cha cha cha with the humungous hippo
I will skip in my box and dance on the ice
And finally put out the simmering fire.

Robyn Munro (9)
Castel Primary School, Castel, Guernsey

The Magic Box

(Based on 'Magic Box' by Kit Wright)

I will put in the box . . .

A rebellious racoon rushing round a rat
A big blue banana balancing on a branch
A pink peapod playing with a pin.

I will put in the box . . .

A drop of indigo-coloured rain
A wall made out of balls
And a brick bouncing on the floor.

I will put in the box . . .

A legendary lake of life
A garden of blue light
And a tropical seed buried in the ground.

My box is fashioned from
Diamonds and pearls and crystals
The lid is created from dragons' scales
And the inside is made from emeralds gleaming in the light.

I shall explore in my box
And live an eternal life of happiness and peace
With the box's love beside me for evermore.

Dylan James (9)
Castel Primary School, Castel, Guernsey

The Magic Box

(Based on 'Magic Box' by Kit Wright)

I will put in the box . . .

A poet's poems placed in a book
Rosie rabbit racing rapidly along the road
A fantastic football flying in the goal.

I will put in the box . . .

A cat chasing a dog
An elephant chasing a mouse
A pig with multicoloured feathers
And a parrot with pink skin and a curly tail.

I will put in the box . . .

A gorgeous Birman cat that can talk every language
A football that can roll anywhere I choose
Absolutely no rules.

My box is fashioned from
Rubies and diamonds around the lid
And a piece of happiness.

I will talk to my cat all day long.

Oliver Toussaint (9)
Castel Primary School, Castel, Guernsey

Boris And The Bear

There once was a boy called Boris
Who'd sneak out and play in the forest
Once he was there
He'd try to trap hare
And look for wild mushrooms and flowers

Now, on his way back to the trap
With mushrooms stuffed in his hat
Seemingly out of thin air
Stood a great grizzly bear
And now there's no sight of dear Boris

His gran and grandpa
Looked for him near and far
And stumbled into the forest
And who should they see
Stuck up a great tree?
But their grandson, dear Boris!

Thomas Upson (8)
Castel Primary School, Castel, Guernsey

If I Could, I Would...

If I could, I would . . .
Bounce on marshmallows
I'd swim in hot chocolate
I'd drink lemonade all day
And I wouldn't have to pay

If I could, I would . . .
Have biscuits for tea
And crisps for my lunch
And my breakfast would be
Chocolate chip cookies, *yummy!*

If I could, I would . . .
In the summer, I'd go to Barbados
In the winter, I'd go to Lapland
I wouldn't have to go to school
Instead, I'd go in the swimming pool!

Sophie Le Feuvre (9)
Castel Primary School, Castel, Guernsey

When Will...?

When will...
Pigs fly?
Angels lie?
Parents understand?

When will...
Sisters stop nagging?
Brothers stop bragging?
Teachers let you off?

When will...
Your alarm stop ringing?
Birds stop singing?
School end at last?

Ruby Davison (8)
Castel Primary School, Castel, Guernsey

Free Ride

Me and my mum went to the fair
She pointed at a ride, right over there
I'd not see a ride like that before
So we went to explore
The ride was so high
It nearly touched the sky
A man at the door, looked up and said
'Hi! Would you like to ride my slide?
If you like, you can have a free ride!'

Erin Harris (7)
Castel Primary School, Castel, Guernsey

Peaceful Daisies

The daisies in the school field
Their petals as white as pearls
Their middles as yellow as bumblebees' stripes
Yet they belong to no baron or earl

The daisies that grow in my garden
How pinkish their petals do grow
In strong winds they roll around like marbles
But in a breeze, they just rock to and fro

The ducks that waddle around in the park
Get the beauty of these all the time
I could wander around all day looking at those
As I'm waiting for it to get dark.

Rebecca Cox (10)
Castel Primary School, Castel, Guernsey

My Dog

My dog is as great as can be,
He is the best dog in the world to me.
He's a family pet,
We all love him so much,
He has the gentlest touch.
He likes to run and jump and play,
He loves to play all day.
My dog is as great as can be,
He is very loyal to me.

Anna Renouf (9)
Castel Primary School, Castel, Guernsey

Rich And Poor

I have a big house, like a castle
And a nice car, as red as fire.

I've got my own butler, as loyal as the king
And a luxury bed, as comfy as Heaven.

I've got all the food I need
And it tastes like Heaven.

I have a gigantic medicine cabinet
As tall as a skyscraper.

I get paid £500 an hour
Plus five diamonds.

I have the nicest stuff
And I've got five Oscars.

Stranger: 'That rich man is the Devil!'

I am as penniless
As a rock.

I am as sick as a germ
And smell like a pig.

I have no job
And bad food that tastes like mud.

I have a wooden house as cold as ice
And up the road is that rich snob.

I have nothing, except for my smelly rags
And that rich snob kicks me all day.

I have no medicine
And one mattress as thin as paper.

Joseph Cowin (10)
Murray's Road School, Douglas, Isle of Man

I Am Cold, You Are Hot

I am cold
My teeth chatter like chatterboxes.

I am cold
My knees knock.

You are hot
You sweat like a pig.

You are hot
You pant like a dog.

I am cold
My ears freeze in the icy wind.

I am cold
My fingers freeze.

You are hot
You get distracted in the blazing warmth.

You are hot
You feel like a fire.

Connor Shakespeare (9)
Murray's Road School, Douglas, Isle of Man

Unusual Days

Tomorrow the gloomy sun will rain
Yesterday the sea will go under water
Today the sun will make dark
And the moon will make light.

Dylan Luke Fearon (9)
Murray's Road School, Douglas, Isle of Man

Anne Frank

During the war and unhappiness
We live in a little annex.
Although we have a fight or two
We still like being here with you.
I am writing a diary about my life
I'm really glad to be alive.

I have a big sister
A mum and dad too
We live with the Van Daans
And Mr Dussel too
We have a lot of helpers
We really wish they'd stay
But they have to go to work
And bring us some food.

I hate hearing bombs at night
But at least we are still alive.
We wonder if the annex is going to burn down
And we will all die.

Hannah Charlotte Cuthbert (9)
Murray's Road School, Douglas, Isle of Man

Loud And Quiet

One morning, I heard a crash,
I heard a clatter,
A scream, a shout,
I heard a deafening cry,
A boom, a bang,
I heard a sound as loud as a monkey,
I heard loud thunder,
Where is all this noise from?

It is peaceful,
No noise,
You could probably hear a snake,
You can hear a pin drop,
It's calm,
Silent as can be,
Very pleasant,
Restful too,
Why is this happening to our town?

Sarah-Jane Catherine Bell (10)
Murray's Road School, Douglas, Isle of Man

Angry And Calm

When I'm angry, I can be mean
When I'm angry, I shout like a lion
When I'm angry, I can be evil!

When I'm calm, I am nice
When I'm calm, I am relaxed
When I'm calm, I am warm, warm, warm!

James Crook (9)
Murray's Road School, Douglas, Isle of Man

Bullying And Friendship

I once was in class
And a girl came in
She's a new girl all right
But a bit of a bully
Her hair was black
Her coat was black
I didn't like the look of her a lot.

But when I got to know her
She was really nice inside
Then she became my best friend
Of all time.

She always laughed
She was always funny
But then she choked
And that was the end
Of my best friend.

Yasmin Bell (9)
Murray's Road School, Douglas, Isle of Man

Dolphin

D ancing on the water
O ut of sight, never to be seen
L oving and beautiful
P leasant and clean
H appy and adorable
I am a whale
N ot really, I'm a cute dolphin!

Gabriella Lulu Swan May Hay (9)
Murray's Road School, Douglas, Isle of Man

Rich And Poor

The rich people are selfish
They have money to burn
It is like they have a money tree
That gives them millions of pounds a day
They have massive houses that they don't need
It is like an elephant, but much, much bigger
They don't give anything to charity
They get all that money for nothing
Like a wild animal being fed.

Poor people don't own a thing, not a penny
It is like a tycoon without a soul
Poor people are people who don't have any houses
And if they do, it is small, like an ant
They wear rags because they can't afford clothes
They beg just for money
They certainly aren't rich.

Robert James Blenkinsop (10)
Murray's Road School, Douglas, Isle of Man

Romance

R omantic nights
O n the round icy moon
M agnificent presents
A mazing honeymoons
N ice and loving
C aring for each other
E xcitement in the air.

Jacob Brand (9)
Murray's Road School, Douglas, Isle of Man

I Hate Sprouts

I hate sprouts
Green, like grass
I hate sprouts
Round, like footballs
I hate sprouts
Full of goodness
I hate sprouts
Good for you
I hate sprouts
Why, oh why, does Mum keep putting them on my plate?
I hate sprouts
One day, when I'm big
I just might try one
I hate sprouts.

Gareth Lee Chilcott (9)
Murray's Road School, Douglas, Isle of Man

Earth And Space

I said hello to an alien,
I couldn't understand,
I boomed my feet,
He didn't say one thing
And shook me by the hand.
I said, 'Hello!'
He looked curious in a way,
He took a breath
And said out loud,
'See you another day!'

Jorja Marie Christian (10)
Murray's Road School, Douglas, Isle of Man

Like And Dislike

I like sleepovers!
I like basketball!
I dislike cheese!
I dislike the wind!
I like parties!
I like cooking!
I dislike spiders!
I dislike bullying!
I like apples!
I like school!
But the best thing of all
Is playing in the pool!

Lucy Banks (10)
Murray's Road School, Douglas, Isle of Man

War And Peace

During peacetime
Everybody is calm and happy,
Everybody is kind to each other,
Everybody's houses aren't very damaged
And all the soldiers are not very tired
And the army has no enemies.

During wartime
There are battles going on all the time,
Soldiers cannot get through the mud,
Bombers taking off every minute,
Tanks easily getting through the mud with soldiers.

Jack Goodwin (10)
Murray's Road School, Douglas, Isle of Man

School

School, school, you can drool
All over your work.

School, school, it's a bore
You can walk straight out of the door.

When you want to play all day
It's school instead of play.

You can't wait until the end of the day . . .
Because it's school!

Rachel Elizabath Crook (9)
Murray's Road School, Douglas, Isle of Man

The Children

He hurts and criticises
He insults and talks in class
He is an ox
And he is as mad as an . . . ogre!

She helps and cares
She rewards and congratulates
She is a fox
She is as clever as a tiger!

Luke Bateman (10)
Murray's Road School, Douglas, Isle of Man

Love

Love is pink like flamingos
It tastes like strawberries from heart-shaped seeds
It smells of wonderful love perfume
It looks like fairies flying
And mermaids swimming round and round
It sounds like music drifting and playing in my head
It feels like floating in the air
That's what love is to me.

Lainna Garcia (8)
Murray's Road School, Douglas, Isle of Man

What Is It?

It's as slow as a snail,
It's as fast as a cheetah,
It's as spotty as a Dalmatian,
It's as stripy as a zebra,
It's as graceful as a swan,
It's as clumsy as a pig,
What is it?
Animals!

Lisa Cross (10)
Murray's Road School, Douglas, Isle of Man

Love Is . . .

Love is happiness
It looks like a massive heart
The colour is rich, bright red
It smells like your favourite perfume
And it feels soft and warm
It sounds like your most happy song
Love tastes like the best sweet you ever had!

Megan Birch (9)
Murray's Road School, Douglas, Isle of Man

Fear!

Fear is black, like murky water
It tastes like over-salted fish
It smells like mouldy potato
It looks like trees with red eyes
It sounds like nails screeching on a chalkboard
It feels cold and lonely.

Anton Ivshin (10)
Murray's Road School, Douglas, Isle of Man

Sadness

Sadness is grey like the clouds
It tastes of saltwater from the sea
It smells like a rotten apple
It looks like a black hole
It sounds like someone crying
It feels like jagged rocks.

Karl Andrew Callister (10)
Murray's Road School, Douglas, Isle of Man

Love

Love is red like our hearts
Love tastes like strawberry sauce
Love smells like a sweet cherry
Love looks like a big cheesy smile
Love sounds like a singing bird
Love feels like happiness.

Hannah Joan Sayle (10)
Murray's Road School, Douglas, Isle of Man

A Year – Haikus

Spring
Baby animals
Smiles are on farmers' faces
Sweet little babies

Summer
Leaves brighten the day
Golden grains cover the shore
Suncream covers you

Autumn
Crispy, crunchy leaves
Freezing weather coming soon
Make use of the warm

Winter
Huge, thick, white blanket
Beautiful icy landscapes
Dull, misty weather.

Ben Holland (9)
Notre Dame Du Rosaire Primary School, St Peter Port, Guernsey

Summer – Haiku

Golden, red skies glow
Beautiful sunsets are here
Start of hot summer . . .

Anasofia Ray (8)
Notre Dame Du Rosaire Primary School, St Peter Port, Guernsey

The Four Seasons – Haikus

Spring
Little lambs playing
Mother hen and brood of chicks
Daffodils in bloom

Summer
Hot, bright summer sun
The sea glitters serenely
Vast, blue, cloudless sky

Autumn
Squirrels scurrying
Hedgehogs rustling in the leaves
Gold, yellow, red, brown

Winter
Pure, white snow falling
Icing sugar on the trees
Delicate snowflakes.

Ellie Holland (10)
Notre Dame Du Rosaire Primary School, St Peter Port, Guernsey

Seasons – Haikus

Spring
Yellow, orange, rose
Out to play, whistling away
Always warm at night

Summer
Hot, hot, very hot
At the beach all day burning
Sea … *no!* Cold, cold, cold

Autumn
Leaves blowing around
At the park the shop is closed
Home, the heater's on

Winter
Wow! It's snowing there
I'm going out, my first time
Can I come in, please?

Esmee Guilbert-Robinson (8)
Notre Dame Du Rosaire Primary School, St Peter Port, Guernsey

A Year – Haikus

Spring
Lambs drinking milk now
Trying to walk around first
Hooray! We did it!

Summer
Sand sticking to me
Sandcastles, spades and buckets
Let's go for a swim . . .

Autumn
Leaves are red and brown
Falling from the trees above
Jump into them . . . *now*

Winter
Snow is around me
Making snowmen and snowballs
Snow is such great fun!

Molly Paul (8)
Notre Dame Du Rosaire Primary School, St Peter Port, Guernsey

My Poem — Haikus

Summer
New greeting season
Opening up mysteries
Of the bright, red sun

Winter
Frozen criminal
Powering snow around you
Cold, unwelcoming

Autumn
Brown trees are left bare
Kids messing up sorted leaves
The smell of bonfires

Spring
Thrilled kids are outside
Enjoying the flowers' bloom
And the bees' buzzing.

Daniel Ray (10)
Notre Dame Du Rosaire Primary School, St Peter Port, Guernsey

Seasons Poem – Haikus

Spring is colourful
Baby animals are born
It is wonderful

Summer is lovely
Nice to sunbathe on the beach
You could get sunburned

Autumn's where leaves blow
And squirrels will hibernate
Hedgehogs can be found

Winter is awesome
It is known for being cold
It's windy outside.

Olivia Le Friec (9)
Notre Dame Du Rosaire Primary School, St Peter Port, Guernsey

Seasons

Winter is so cool
You can play with lots of snow
And hot chocolate too

Summer is pretty
People sunbathe on the beach
There are lots of pets

Autumn is brown, red
Standing in the windy weather
Legs are shivering.

Christina Allen (9)
Notre Dame Du Rosaire Primary School, St Peter Port, Guernsey

Back To School

B ye-bye summer holidays
A u revoir to sun
C heerio to lazy ways
K iss goodbye to fun

T eachers call us into class
O ur faces filled with dread

S hould have brought my homework in
C an't I go back to bed?
H ome time's always hours away
O ur school's fantastic, but
O utside is where I long to be
L aughing like a nut!

Tove Barnes (10)
Notre Dame Du Rosaire Primary School, St Peter Port, Guernsey

Back To School

B ack to school
A rt, maths and ICT
C oming in, I see the tidy pencil pots
K aty's forgotten her homework and oh no - so have I!

T here are tons of people falling
O utside - yelling and wailing

S ome teacher will
C ome soon, but maybe they might be put off by the rain
H undreds of children are late for school, their answer is
O h, my mum forgot to wake me up
O h, there was lots of traffic. The teacher says, 'What road'
L ots of people are thinking: and it's going to take a while!

Matilda Ayres (9)
Notre Dame Du Rosaire Primary School, St Peter Port, Guernsey

Back To School

B ags are heavy
A nother day
C ome and play
K knowledge comes

T imes tables
O ne, two, three

S kipping games
C lassrooms full
H omework done
O verjoyed to leave
O n my way
L eaving time.

Nicole Upton (10)
Notre Dame Du Rosaire Primary School, St Peter Port, Guernsey

Back To School

B ells are ringing for school
A lways rushing around
C hristmas has gone, sadly it's school again
K atie's a bit late for school

T ime to work everyone, *oh no*
O h no, sloppy science

S inging practise later
C lassroom is empty, because it's lunch
H olidays are over sadly
O h, more work, work and more work
O h yes, no homework at all
L et's go home, *hooray!*

Hannelore Williams-Reid (8)
Notre Dame Du Rosaire Primary School, St Peter Port, Guernsey

Back To School

B all time is fun
A nd lots of friends to play with
C heating at my homework or
K icking people at school is not what you should do

T rying to work hard every day
O n and on having homework, you see

S houting, screaming, lots of noise every playtime too
C lapping, singing, maths
H anging about every playtime
O ut and about when it's home time
O h, what is it like to be at school
L ike everything!

Elizabeth Correia (7)
Notre Dame Du Rosaire Primary School, St Peter Port, Guernsey

Journey To The Beach

I went to the beach for some shade
And saw a big, scary crab,
So I caught him with my bucket and spade
And he ended up giving me a jab!

I went to the beach for some sun
I took my bathers and wrap,
I built a castle for fun
Then I lay down and had a nap!

Daniel Le Cheminant (10)
SS Mary & St Michael RC Primary School, St Sampsons, Guernsey

The Haunted House

You step inside the broken door
And hear nothing, but the creak of the floor,
You hear footsteps down below
Down where nobody can go.

You shake, turn and glance
Around you, dark shadows dance,
You go in the cellar to take a look
You see a battered skeleton hung on a hook.

You bang into someone, but there's nobody there
You shake with fear and stop and stare,
You hear a door open and slam shut
You feel sick in your gut.

You run out of the front door
There's no horror anymore,
You talk and hear horrible groans
You look at yourself and see nothing but bones!

Joshua Ozanne
SS Mary & St Michael RC Primary School, St Sampsons, Guernsey

Spring

S ummer's on its way
P etals appearing on the flowers
R ainy days now and then
I ndoor play, outdoor play
N ests are being built
G reen leaves are growing.

Aidan Brookes (10)
SS Mary & St Michael RC Primary School, St Sampsons, Guernsey

The Haunted House

As you enter the creepy, haunted house
Be sure not to step on the mouse,
You enter the dark house by the door
Where there are dangers many more.

You are in the house, it's pitch-black
You shriek at the sight of a creepy cat,
There is a massive spiral staircase
You notice something weird at your face.

There is a big painting of a lobster
Then out of it, comes a scary monster!
You just make it, you keep your life
You have just been trapped in a pit of mice!

At the corner of your eye, you see the treasure
With every corner, the right measure
You are pleased with yourself, you feel good
You leave with your black and white hood!

Nathan Austin (10)
SS Mary & St Michael RC Primary School, St Sampsons, Guernsey

Sport

S liding
P enguins
O ften
R esemble
T oboggans.

Aaron Jordan Coulson (11)
SS Mary & St Michael RC Primary School, St Sampsons, Guernsey

Easter

Soon, it is going to be Easter
There will be lots of chocolate eggs in the shops
I wonder if we will see the Easter bunny?
Because I like the way that he hops!

I love going on egg hunts
Looking for eggs in the trees
I wonder if there are any by this tree stump?
I hope that I don't bang my knees!

I have coloured in my Easter bunny picture
I have remembered to hand it in
It's really bright and colourful
I really hope that I win!

Zeke Boyce (10)
SS Mary & St Michael RC Primary School, St Sampsons, Guernsey

Birthday

B alloons that float
I cing on the colourful cake
R ainbow streamers shoot across the table
T he candles flicker in the dark
H e sits in the birthday seat, making a wish
D oes he get what he wants?
A laptop, with lots of memory
Y es he does and he has a great day!

Jordan Redwood (10)
SS Mary & St Michael RC Primary School, St Sampsons, Guernsey

Tigers

Tigers are vicious
Tigers are fierce
They hunt in the night
And can kill with one bite!

Liam John Concannon (10)
SS Mary & St Michael RC Primary School, St Sampsons, Guernsey

The Ocean's Secrets

I swim through the billowing ocean,
Everything is seemingly lifeless above the surface.
Beneath the raging waves,
The excitement begins.
Small fish streak through the water,
Hiding from predators in ancient wrecks.
Flatfish glide lazily along the seabed,
They camouflage themselves, waiting for their prey.
Giant starfish creep slowly across the rocks, looking for food,
Nearer the surface, shoals of fish swim hurriedly.
As dolphin circle them,
They dive in to grab a fish that has strayed from the group.
A drab and dreary fish swims on its own,
Across the colourful reef.
Suddenly, an ominous shape appears from the darkness,
The fish vanishes into the shark's strong, powerful jaws.

Kelly Dixon (10)
St John's School, St John, Jersey

I Am Diving

I am diving, going lower and lower
I am going to a bottomless ocean
I see creatures that are unknown
I am flowing with the elegant sea
The brilliant reef below me shares amazing creatures
That enjoy swimming with me
Suddenly, a giant ray comes gliding above me
I watch its elegance and grace
I look at my oxygen tank
I don't have as much time as I need
To see this amazing and beautiful world below.

Dylan Hopwood (11)
St John's School, St John, Jersey

Under The Sea

The billowing waves crash
Against the wrecked, abandoned boat
The shore seems deserted
As the force of the sea pushes me forward
The misty sky causes the sea
To become rougher for me and my stranded friends
The gigantic swell of the sea
Pushes the seaweed to the shore
Then, the dark beast of the sea comes for me
But I dodge away, out-smarting him
He continues to lurk, waiting for his unsuspecting prey.

Matthew Allo (11)
St John's School, St John, Jersey

Seascape!

S un shines on the water, making it glisten like crystal
E very bird in the sky is squawking, although I can hear them
 I can't see them
A cross the beach people talk and intersperse with laughter
S oft, warm sand lies beneath my feet
C rashing, the waves come in, frothy and cold
A t the beach, people lie on towels with the hot sun shining on them
P eeping behind rocks, crabs scatter and scurry
E very rock pool has a variety of creatures living in them happily
 and waiting for the sea to come in and replenish their habitat.

Dana Stamps (11)
St John's School, St John, Jersey

Deepest Ocean

Watch the white horses jumping
Over the seas
Dodging billowing waves
Dolphins sing to each other
As they play
Fish swim in and out of the seaweed
As they go to and fro
The deepest ocean isn't just an ocean
It is magical and amazing!

Kira Jayne Mitchell (10)
St John's School, St John, Jersey

A World Of Colour

The crystal-clear, blue sea crashes powerfully
On the grainy sand
The baby turtle makes his escape
Surviving a near impossible challenge
I enter the predatory waters and gaze at this bold, colourful world
New, exotic fish dive swiftly around me
A bright display of colour moves before me
Swiftly, smoothly, cautiously and powerfully
Visions I will never forget.

Cameron Queree (10)
St John's School, St John, Jersey

The Ocean

T he twirling, turbulent, threatening sea
H orrible, hazy, hostile sea
E xuberant environment, sea

O bliterating ocean waves
C alm, crystal, curl-free ocean
E ndangered, enthralling, extravagant
A dmiring creatures dive deep, deep in the ocean
N aturally neat ocean floor.

Remy Hidrio (10)
St John's School, St John, Jersey

Seascape

S eaweed crunches beneath my feet, hard, brittle and sharp
E ar-shattering cries of seagulls among the grey, towering rocks
A gigantic wave encompasses my shoulder
S alty sea water all over my wind-burned face
C rashing waves on the rocks, fill the treasure-filled pools
A dog barking endlessly for its ball to be thrown
P eople talk and laugh in the friendly, lively café above
E mptiness in my head, it seems to be just me and the sea!

Tamsin D'Orleans (10)
St John's School, St John, Jersey

The Jungle

In the jungle, the trees stand very high in the sky
Which the monkeys climb
The birds fly high over
The snakes slither around them
That's what happens in the jungle
The maple river runs through
Which the bridge runs over and the monkeys race across
There is a boat in the middle of the maple river
The monkeys race over the bendy branches
Of the trees with the maple leaves
Diddy Kong, Donkey Kong and Funky Kong
Jump from tree to tree
The maple piranhas watch the monkeys race across the bridge
Which goes over the maple river
Where the maple piranhas watch from
That's what happens in the jungle.

Joel Fallon (8)
St Martin's Primary School, St Martin, Jersey

Two Minutes' Silence

Close your eyes,
Lay your head,
Think of all the people
Who are dead.
The people were brave,
The people were strong,
The people were mighty
And not wrong.
Why are there wars?
They should stop now!
The only problem is - *how?*
How? How?
The poppies shall not be forgotten,
To remember the brave,
You shouldn't forget them,
Or wash them away.
If it wasn't for them, Britain would not be free,
Freedom is what they want
And that is what it shall be.
In the future, war shall be questioned,
People would say:
'What is war? It's never been mentioned.'
Close your eyes,
Lay your head,
Think of all the people
Who are now dead.

Jack Evans (8)
St Martin's Primary School, St Martin, Jersey

Who's That?

Who's that?
That's Uncle Gerry
And that's Gran,
Drinking sherry.

Who's that?
Auntie Debbie,
Who's that?
Baby Sebbie.

Who's that?
Cousin Dan,
Playing with
A pot and pan.

Who's that?
Auntie Zoey,
At the zoo,
Patting a joey.

Who's that?
You and your first meal,
Eating like
A moody seal.

Alice Mollet (10)
St Martin's Primary School, St Martin, Jersey

Who's That?

Who's that?
That's Uncle Billy,
Yes, my uncle
Being silly.

Who's that?
Uncle Dave,
He's catching
A wave.

Who's that?
Uncle Dave,
He is near a bear,
He's very brave.

Who's that?
Your cousin Kelly,
What is she eating?
That's green jelly.

Who's that
In the bed?
Turn it around,
It's Uncle Ted.

Dylan Buesnel (11)
St Martin's Primary School, St Martin, Jersey

Experiences Of Swimming

My hands split the water as a dagger does skin,
Fish flit around me,
Silver streaks of moonlight in the dark water, the night sky,
As I dive deeper, crabs skitter over the gravel,
Chickens on the busy farmyard of the seabed,
A dark shape looms up in front of me,
A coral reef!
The fish,
Now tropical, flit,
Like flies,
Amongst the many-coloured kingdom of the coral,
I resurface,
Look up at the night sky,
The two realms of sky and water are identical,
Fish and stars,
Water and night sky,
I am free,
Nobody and nothing but sky and water around me,
All is quiet,
I am peaceful as the water engulfs me once again.

Maya Walton (8)
St Martin's Primary School, St Martin, Jersey

Nile

N ile flowing fast
I t is nice in the Nile
L urking beneath are crocodiles
E eek! I'm not going in!

Harrison Lee Carlyon (8)
St Martin's Primary School, St Martin, Jersey

Pyramid

P is for P yramid, old and scary
  dark and cold and very steamy
Y is for Y ucky, creepy-crawlies
  and solid, silky sand
R is for R aining, dribbles pattering
  on the top roof of the pyramid
A is for old, A ncient Egypt
  that was brought from the dead
M is for M iles and miles away
  the pyramids go over the dusty sands
I is for I vy on the sheds
  of the pyramids
D is for D angerous, deadly mummies
  that are brought from the dead.

Skye Fox (7)
St Martin's Primary School, St Martin, Jersey

The Sea

You can swim in the sea
That's the place for me
Walk on the beach
Eating a peach
Go in deep
Where it's very steep
Play a game
But don't get the blame
Sing a song
But don't take long!

Rebecca Renouard (8)
St Martin's Primary School, St Martin, Jersey

Animal Communication!

C ats are cool, but not in a pool
O ctopus are wide, not inside
M onkeys are nuts when they're in huts
M ice are ice and nice
U nicorns fly high in the sky
N o animals are allowed in here
I wouldn't think a lot, I would
C ommunicate
A nimals communicate
T o the jungle, to the far sea, animals communicate
I can see
O n a day, bright and clear, you can hear communication
N o one knows what they say, but they do.

Lucy May Hilton (7)
St Martin's Primary School, St Martin, Jersey

WWII

Bombs, guns
Scary air raids
Loud planes
German soldiers
Being mean
Shocking sounds
Small shelters
Army tanks
Shooting bombs
Horrible sights
WWII stop!

Joel Lucas-Villar (8)
St Martin's Primary School, St Martin, Jersey

Poetry Explorers – British Isles

When I Moved School

When I moved to a new school,
I missed my friends back at Sciennes,
I missed Aleena in her jeans,
I missed Hazel,
Not the tree,
But my worst enemy!
I didn't miss the concrete playground,
Cos one pound crisp packets were on the ground,
I do miss having half a day,
Every finishing off Friday!
Thursday was my favourite day,
We sometimes made things out of clay!

Amy Claxton (8)
St Martin's Primary School, St Martin, Jersey

The Sea

The sea is blue, with lots of creatures
Crabs *snip, snip, snip!*
Starfish are very rare.

Fish swim and have fun
Be nice to everyone.

Waves are curling up the beach
And surfers boogie on their surfboards.

Boats racing past
With people laughing and having fun
Have a good time everyone!

Chantal Le Rossignol (7)
St Martin's Primary School, St Martin, Jersey

Weather Poem

Snow is falling far, far through the night
When the wind blows, the snow drifts away
And no longer will be snow
Rain *pitter-patters* all on the roofs
Out comes the sun and dries up all the rain
Today the sun is shining
It's really great
The night is coming and the day is going
All the people are asleep now
So I must end now
But I will see you again.

Sophie Venton (8)
St Martin's Primary School, St Martin, Jersey

Forever Friends

Friends are forever
Not never, never, never
In our class, you should not have one, not two, but 26!
Don't call them names, let them join in games
Play for long
Until they are gone
And nothing will go wrong
Because that's what friends are for
Friends are forever
Not never, never, never!

Leanne Carroll (8)
St Martin's Primary School, St Martin, Jersey

I Dream Of The Jungle

I close my eyes,
Right in front of me, I find
A tiger ready to pounce on me!
I quickly run away!
I see all the tropical colours as I go past,
Suddenly, I hear a hissing sound,
There are snakes spiralling around my legs!
Then I suddenly wake up screaming, in the middle of the night,
I found out it was just a dream of the jungle!

Lilly Simon Heslam (7)
St Martin's Primary School, St Martin, Jersey

The Sea

Blue water with lots of bubbles
Fish in the water, swimming around
Crabs pinching in the water, below the blue, blue sea
Sharks lurking around and around
Coral reefs in the blue sea
Piranhas swimming all together by the seaweed
Caves with octopus with their scary eight legs in the blue sea
Turtles flapping their flippers
Blue water.

Brody Boleat (8)
St Martin's Primary School, St Martin, Jersey

Egypt

Perfect pyramids piled up high
Golden glory up, up high
Black land, red, fierce, flooding too!
Shadoofs carry water up and down
Creating lots of life
Slaves work hard to earn their right
Pharaohs rule for many years
The Nile flows down Egypt
Feluccas sail up and down the mighty Nile.

Patrick Claxton (7)
St Martin's Primary School, St Martin, Jersey

Remembrance Day!

Relatives died
Children cried

Mother stayed up all night
Thinking of a fight

Men were very scared
But they still cared

Everyone was granted freedom.

Shauna Danvill (9)
St Martin's Primary School, St Martin, Jersey

Mythicals

Mythicals, mythicals, let's talk about them
Unicorns dashing and flashing, prancing and dancing in the field
Fairies fluttering and muttering as they work
Goblins and gremlins being so naughty to unicorns and fairies
Let's go to the Pole, don't forget the coal
Watch out for the prints, that's one big hint
Mythicals, mythicals, we've finished talking about them
See you again, now and then!

Tegan Jade Parker (7)
St Martin's Primary School, St Martin, Jersey

Mythical Creatures

Unicorn wonder, spirits bright,
Unicorn wonder, the horn makes a light.
Dragons are fierce, dragons are brave,
If you go near them it will be your grave.
You would think that mermaids were nice,
But actually, they would kill mice.
They would break your bones and makes you moan,
You would think that mermaids were nice.

Cleo Leather (7)
St Martin's Primary School, St Martin, Jersey

Ancient Egypt

P retty pyramids of Giza
Y ou're in *ancient Egypt*
R amases the Great is ruling now
A ncient Egypt is the best
M ummification is now
I n ancient Egypt, the pharaohs were great
D angerous creatures lurk in the deep of the Nile
S ome pretty pyramids of Giza.

Flora Leather (7)
St Martin's Primary School, St Martin, Jersey

Pyramids

P yramids are steep
Y ou don't want to go in there
R unning everywhere trying to find an exit
A re you going in there? Yes
M ummies are everywhere trying to get out of the bandages
I don't want to go in there again
D istances everywhere, I'm lost!

Deacon Wilson (7)
St Martin's Primary School, St Martin, Jersey

Hobbies

Hobbies
Hopping, skipping
Swimming, riding, racing
Tumbles, turns, tennis, tricks
Netball and football
Basketball looping
Swooping.

Daniella Le Beurrier (7)
St Martin's Primary School, St Martin, Jersey

Sun

Sun
Bright light
Fright, dry, hot
The sun with us, the sun without us
Sun goes down
Moon comes
Up.

Leonel Camacho (8)
St Martin's Primary School, St Martin, Jersey

Pyramids

The pyramids shine like the sun
Slaves built the pyramids as smooth as they could
The pyramids have a reflection in the Nile
The pyramid's top shines like the sun
Slaves built the pyramids as smooth as they could
The pyramids have a reflection in the Nile.

Lily-Mae Fry (7)
St Martin's Primary School, St Martin, Jersey

The Sea

Salty water
Whales singing
Dolphins dining
Mermaids splashing
Seaweed smelling
Pretty coral.

Katie Marett (8)
St Martin's Primary School, St Martin, Jersey

Games

G reat fun
A musing
M y favourite - 'Guns Of The Patriots'
E xciting
S ports games for Dad.

Callum Du Heaume (7)
St Martin's Primary School, St Martin, Jersey

Eight-Legged Friend

Spider
Crawling around
Eight-legged, hairy friend
Hunting for prey around the ground
Arachnid.

Calvin Carroll (10)
St Martin's Primary School, St Martin, Jersey

Flying - Cinquain

Flying
Flying so high
Unicorn flap your wings
And fly round the world very fast
Flight ends.

Charlie Lucas (7)
St Martin's Primary School, St Martin, Jersey

Willow

Loving, cuddly
Snoring softly, sound asleep
Playing with her stick
The garden's hers - happy, free
Scared of boots, but glad to be!

Charis Renouf (11)
St Martin's Primary School, St Martin, Jersey

The Sea – Cinquain

The sea
Salty water
Whale calling, whale singing
Dolphins diving, splashing water
Pretty.

Molly Bettencourt (7)
St Martin's Primary School, St Martin, Jersey

Space – Cinquain

Rockets
In space zooming
Through the universe with
The planets and the moon seeing
Stars too.

Max Roberts (7)
St Martin's Primary School, St Martin, Jersey

Space

S pace is outside the world
P eaceful in space
A liens live on Mars
C hina's Great Wall can be seen from space
E xplorers can go to the moon.

Emily Le Gallais (7)
St Martin's Primary School, St Martin, Jersey

The Jungle – Cinquain

Speed rain,
All animals
Fast snakes hiss all day long,
All rain and animals and snakes,
Jungle!

George Cousins (8)
St Martin's Primary School, St Martin, Jersey

Karting

Karting
Whirling, ripping
Speeding, racing, spinning
I flick the button, great, now go
Go karting!

Sienna Denny Mallen (11)
St Martin's Primary School, St Martin, Jersey

Science – Cinquain

Science
Bones with muscles
Skeletons and a skull
Moving and growing up and down
Humans.

Ross Lawless (7)
St Martin's Primary School, St Martin, Jersey

Penguin

The emperor penguin,
Standing tall in frozen land,
Standing tall and black,
They rule the frozen land,
He's as cool as cool can be.

Mark Marett (11)
St Martin's Primary School, St Martin, Jersey

Light

Light
Shining bright
Glowing, blazing, glaring
High up in the ceiling above
Limelight.

Lucy Le Gallais (11)
St Martin's Primary School, St Martin, Jersey

My Mummy

Mother of four kids,
My mummy is always there,
She's as gentle as Polo,
Soft and kind, she's my hero,
She is as bright as the moon.

Courtney Jane Carrel (11)
St Martin's Primary School, St Martin, Jersey

Nile

N ile is flowing fast
I would go on a ferry
L ong, long Nile, flowing fast
E xcellent Egypt.

Joshua Michael Le Gallais (7)
St Martin's Primary School, St Martin, Jersey

Space – Haiku

Round the world I go
Going through the Milky Way
I will never stop.

Brandon Le Rossignol (8)
St Martin's Primary School, St Martin, Jersey

Daddy

Dad, I dearly love you
You've really got is sussed.

You're the one and only man,
A girl can ever trust.

If you weren't in my life,
I don't know what I'd do.

If you weren't here today,
I would never know.

There will never be a man,
I'll love more than you, Dad.

You're the one standing by my side,
Stopping me from turning bad.

I need you by my side,
I need you in my life.

And there's also another girl,
The one you call your wife.

You're my light, my guide,
By your rules I abide.

A guardian angel on Earth,
Yes, you're really worth.

All the cups of tea,
All the 'Honey, will you do this for me?'

I hope I have explained,
You're like the roof when it rained.

A guardian angel, watching over me,
We're an item - we're a 'we'.

Dad, my angel, my white dove,
You, I truly, dearly, love.

Orla McMullan (11)
St Mary's RC Primary School, Douglas, Isle of Man

Wedding Ring

An old chain
Hung there, thousands of years ago
Married to the sea
A symbol of their marriage
To you and me

Like a wedding ring
An anchor point for years and years connected
Seaweed flung onto the old wedding ring
But never is despair

The slimy green seaweed
Different textures of life
Dry and wet
Swung onto the old chain
With the strain of the sea
Pulling it away and then tugging it back

The frozen rain, as cold as ice
In the bitter winter
The howling wind
And multicoloured leaves fall on the worn
Wedding ring

The chirps of new life
Being born in the spring
Sun rises up
As hot as an oven

And then the poor, old wedding ring
Finally detached from the sea
Alone for evermore
For thousands of years.

Georgina Bourne (11)
St Michael's School, St Saviour, Jersey

The Shining Sun

When I shine on the bay,
I create smiles on faces,
People are happy,
If they are happy,
So am I.

When I shine on the bay,
I have the ability
To melt ice creams!
If people lie beneath me for too long,
I'll burn them!
They may not be so happy then.

When I shine on the bay,
I can make the sea glow,
I can warm the lapping waves,
Turning the sea into a giant bath,
Right before your eyes!

But,
When I decide to leave the bay
And the sea grows dark and menacing,
The crashing waves upon the shore,
Make people go away -
Unless, my friend, the moon,
Comes out to light up the bay.

Angus Drummond (9)
St Michael's School, St Saviour, Jersey

Poetry Explorers – British Isles

The Ancient Castle

Many years ago, I saw
Smoking ships sinking,
Blood bursting barbarically
And ravenous rifles.

Many years ago, I heard
The war cries of the ghastly French,
The shouts of pain from sailors
And the light tap of the general giving his last second.

Many years ago, I felt
The slight pain of my ridge of rock breaking off from cannon fire,
A dense thick blanket of smoke slid over me
And the sheer cold of the stormy battlefield.

Many years ago, I smelt
Burning from the villages below,
Gunpowder from the cannons of enemy ships
And the rotting corpses of enemy soldiers.

Many years ago, I tasted
The water of the rain from the storm,
The burn of blazing fire
And blood dripping off dead men hanging on me.

Now the old days are over,
Finally, my ancient rock and form can rest in peace.

Tate Spurling (9)
St Michael's School, St Saviour, Jersey

Seasons

In winter, I can hear
The rush of the white horses charging in,
The wind howling, like a dog at night,
Children screaming, trying not to get wet
And the seagulls in their woolly feather fleeces.

In spring, I can see
A couple of swimmers in the water,
Spindrift sprouting upon the sand,
The shining sun starts appearing
And the white horses begin to gallop away.

In summer, I can feel
Hot sand between my toes,
The warm sea curdling around my ankles,
Cold ice cream dripping down my face
And the heat of the blazing sun.

In autumn, I can sense
The wind is getting stronger,
There are no flowers, as far as I can see
And all the cafés are packing away
Because winter is on its way.

Emma Banks (11)
St Michael's School, St Saviour, Jersey

Rozel

I can feel the sand squelching beneath my toes,
Yet, I'm not alone,
I feel like the sand is watching me,
This sand is filled with pain,
Yet filled with knowledge,
It could tell stories of everyone's journeys.

Plastic buoys floating lazily in the calm sea,
But when the sea is playful, the buoys surf the waves,
I can smell the salt hiding beneath the natural roller coaster,
I can touch the smooth surface
And the shiny seaweed resting, like a cosy blanket.

The boats could tell joyful stories of all the sea voyages,
They feel pain - the rocks slicing into the shiny plastic,
From a mile away, you can hear the ship's cries pleading to go home.

The lobster pots witness the cries of dying fish,
Though it must feel glad to help all of these hungry sailors,
Keeping their hard-earned treasure.

Emilie Lindsay (11)
St Michael's School, St Saviour, Jersey

A Beach At Sunset

A million shades of colours
From soft mauves to startling scarlet
To peaches and sky-blues
Like a florist's shop in summer
The sun, a luminous yellow beach ball
That was kicked up high in the sky
But never came down.

The waves are white horses
Galloping in from their time at sea
Soon to go out again, as free as a dolphin
Jumping high out of the cool, blue water
Spraying foam in all directions.

In the fading light, you can spot
A huge flock of swallows beginning
Their life-threatening voyage south
For the cold, brittle winter.
All is calm and peaceful.

Jemima O'Connell (10)
St Michael's School, St Saviour, Jersey

Under The Sea

From under the sea, I hear
Laughter and happiness,
Frozen high, suspended, I see multicoloured figures,
As well as shimmering reflections of bright houses.

From under the sea, I feel
Included in everything going on,
Trapped by walls and rocks surrounding me,
Every now and then, seaweed tickles me as I swim by.

From under the sea, I see
The castle standing proud and admired,
People running on the soft, silky sand,
Buses and cars zoom past.

In my watery world, I try to keep safe,
Not to get caught by a big net,
For I am only a little fish
And this has always been my wish.

Hollie Hemaya (9)
St Michael's School, St Saviour, Jersey

The Sea

The creak of ropes straining,
The roaring of waves smashing,
Sea walls seem to shudder
Under the impact of water,
The taste of salty sea, as bitter as lemon,
The smell of oil leaking, like smoke pluming,
The colours of different ropes,
As bright as those in a rainbow,
The small ocean slopes getting ever deeper,
Rocks smashing the walls,
Like ammunition being fired,
The smell of seaweed,
As strong as that of dead fish,
The pale petrol fumes from boats,
Hanging in the air,
Like a faint mist,
These are my favourite features of the sea.

James Unwin (10)
St Michael's School, St Saviour, Jersey

Home

Every time I take a few steps, I create a new nation,
I feel the texture of the sand between my toes,
The sea almost reaches my feet, but runs away again,
The seaweed layers the beach, like a scarf in the winter
                                               to keep it warm,
The wind shouts at my face and pulls back my hair,
Feeling like a mischievous child knotting it up,
I can smell the faint rotting of dead fish,
I can hear the shrieking of seagulls, like a thousand sports
                                         whistles blowing all at once,
I take a dip in the sea and feel like I'm on a roller coaster
                                         from the rolling waves,
Boats bash against the shore, like punching holes in the rocks,
For all this, the beach is home.

Georgia Clews (11)
St Michael's School, St Saviour, Jersey

The Truthful Boat

As classic or ancient or grand as I may be,
That is not anything as beautiful as love.

As responsible or royal as I may be,
That does not beat the giggling of a small child at the beach.

As respected or proud as I may be,
That does not beat helpful people, or the sound of caring people.

You do not know how I hate to see the grey of arguments,
But the colours of friendship are treasured by me.

Elizabeth Baker (9)
St Michael's School, St Saviour, Jersey

The Magical Doorway

Where will it take you?
This magical doorway,
This medieval portal to your dreams,
Will it take you to a view point, where archers awaited,
For a target to eliminate on the endless battlefield below?
Will it take you to a prison in the depths of the castle,
Where prisoners rattle their chains all day long?
Will it take you to a jousting competition,
Where horses charge and knights fight?
Or will it take you to the tourist attraction it is today?
Perched upon the sandy bay.

Benedict Jones (10)
St Michael's School, St Saviour, Jersey

Horses' Rap

We're the horses,
We're the horses,
We go through the big towns,
We find hungry clowns!

We're the horses,
We're the horses,
We like to eat green grass,
We don't like to eat last!

We're the horses,
We're the horses
And that's that!

Christopher Milon (8)
St Saviour's School, St Saviour, Jersey

Horses Rap

We're the horses,
We're the horses,
We gallop through the filthy towns,
We frown at the ugly clowns!

We're the horses,
We're the horses,
We love to eat
Their scrumptious Shredded Wheat,
We step on their stinky feet!

We're the horses,
We're the horses,
We love to jump high jumps,
When we eat our dinners,
We get a bit plump!

We're the horses,
We're the horses,
When we get fed,
We can never fit in our beds!

We're the horses,
We're the horses,
We love to oversleep,
But when we do, our riders weep!

We're the horses,
We're the horses,
We're the horses
And we love to eat loads of courses!

Cerys Griffiths (9) & Alana Ricou (8)
St Saviour's School, St Saviour, Jersey

Hamster Rap

We're the hamsters,
We're the hamsters,
We nibble our metal bars,
We hate the really noisy cars!

We're the hamsters,
We're the hamsters,
We bite them at night,
We give them a huge fright!

We're the hamsters,
We're the hamsters,
We are a cute pet,
But we hate the big scary vet!

We're the hamsters,
We're the hamsters,
We eat their brown nuts,
We give them big nasty cuts!

We're the hamsters,
We're the hamsters,
We tiptoe through the creaky hard floor
And we scamper through the big brown door!

We're the hamsters,
We're the hamsters,
We're the hamsters
And that's that!

Tianne Guillaume & Lara Peters (8)
St Saviour's School, St Saviour, Jersey

Mice Rap

We're the mice,
We're the mice,
We jump on their heads,
We bite them in their white beds!

We're the mice,
We're the mice,
We drink out the water bowl,
We bite the big, hairy mole!

We're the mice,
We're the mice,
We steal their black books,
We whack the silly cooks!

We're the mice,
We're the mice,
We are completely white.
We hunt in the night!!

We're the mice,
We're the mice,
We bite their round nose
And soak them with a green water hose!

We're the mice,
We're the mice,
We're the mice
And that's nice!

Ellie Carré (8)
St Saviour's School, St Saviour, Jersey

The Jack Russell Rap

We're the Jack Russells,
We're the Jack Russells,
We kill the mice,
We eat the dice,
Although it doesn't taste nice!

We're the Jack Russells,
We're the Jack Russells,
We're always mighty,
We're on the hunt nightly!

We're the Jack Russells,
We're the Jack Russells,
We kill the rats
And stop the cats,
We chase the bats!

We're the Jack Russells,
We're the Jack Russells
And we're the best!

Tillie Jones (8)
St Saviour's School, St Saviour, Jersey

Happy Bunny

B unny eats carrots
U nder the chair
N o
N o
Y awning with his happy mouth.

Christopher Henthorn (6)
Scoill Phurt le Moirrey, Port St Mary, Isle of Man

The Hungry Cheetah

C amouflaged in long grass
H e pounces fast
E xcellent predator
E ars are excellent at hearing
T racking people and animal smells
A ttacks with his sharp, pointed claws
H e's proud when he has caught an animal to chew.

Charlie Davidson (11)
Scoill Phurt le Moirrey, Port St Mary, Isle of Man

A Giraffe In Africa

G inger-brown skin
I n the waterhole
R unning through the dry land
A soft brush back
F eet run fast
F lapping ears from the sun
E ating leaves.

Christian Lockerby (8)
Scoill Phurt le Moirrey, Port St Mary, Isle of Man

Fluffy's Day Out

R abbit called Fluffy
A lways likes a cuddle
B iting on carrots
B obby tail
I n the bush
T witching her ears and nose.

Mark Copley (9)
Scoill Phurt le Moirrey, Port St Mary, Isle of Man

Tyson

C ats don't go on trains
A lways drink milk
T yson.

Harvey Shimmin (9)
Scoill Phurt le Moirrey, Port St Mary, Isle of Man

Tiger

Prowling through the grass
Comes a carnivorous beast
Stalking its doomed prey
A lonely male antelope
Looking for its long-lost calf.

Sam Philpot (10)
Victoria College Preparatory School, St Helier, Jersey

Hoover

Silently, sleeping slowly in the cupboard, waiting for a chance,
To go around the house making it cleaner,
Wait! There is a light, a tiny glimmer of hope,
I am nervously shaking as much as a newborn puppy,
Yes, the door is slowly opening and she is taking me out,
Plugging me in and turning me on.

I go around eating, sucking, destroying all dust,
So much, I nearly go bust,
Now, I'm going as fast as a cheetah,
Me, Hoover, a racing driver zipping,
Zooming through here and there,
So fast, I could outrun a polar bear.

I jump with joy, as I zoom over the carpet,
I vacuum it so hard, I nearly part it!
Quickly, sprinting to the kitchen -
But no! It has bumpy tiles!

I'm half broken, bumping over them,
My nightmare . . . but then suddenly, it's over,
Up the stairs, a gigantic mountain, up and down,
Crashing all the way,
I've almost got too much pressure,
I can only hold a small bit more!

Wait - they've noticed! Now they're quickly emptying me,
Phew! That was close! I nearly went *poof!*
Now, back to work . . .
I've practically finished the house and yes,
That's the last room, my lap record,
I'm done, at last, dancing with joy.

But for me, it's back to the cold cupboard,
Where I silently think about being a racing driver
And I'll try and beat that record next time.

Alexander Clarke (11)
Victoria College Preparatory School, St Helier, Jersey

Mr Apple Pie

The slice of apple pie, he's so juicy and sweet,
Swimming in a lake of custard.
He is my favourite treat,
Never, ever is he sour and hard.

He is nice and tender,
My mouth becomes so dry.
Never do I falter,
To stuff him down, if I didn't - I would die!

As he slides down my throat,
He bumps and bumps,
Then does a big hoot
And at the end, he tremendously jumps.

He swirled and twirled,
Round my stomach.
So fast, I nearly hurled,
Like I do when I have haddock.

I was sad that he had gone,
Whipping my finger in the lake of custard.
Next, I ate Mr Chocolate Bonbon,
Then I felt a thump in my stomach.

It was Mr Apple Pie,
Still alive in there!
He didn't want to die -
I didn't care!

Then I lurched,
He ran quickly up and up,
He was free,
Running wild, like a little pup.

William Speck (11)
Victoria College Preparatory School, St Helier, Jersey

Golf Ball

As I crouch anxiously in the devious, dark machine,
I am waiting for someone kind to pay.
I'm patiently sitting, wondering and thinking quite happily,
I'm first in the never-ending long line ready to roll.
I hear the deafening *clunk* of the dreaded machine,
The huge barrier drops slowly, clicks suddenly,
Then rises without warning behind me.
I'm disguised in the crooked basket by all my supportive friends,
Being carried at great speed to the brand new driving bay.
With anticipation, we start to talk about who's gonna go.
As we all roll slowly to the rusty old rack,
I start to laugh uncontrollably with excitement,
Jonnie is first to go . . . . he says his last words,
But I realise that the terrifying time is ticking.
It's nearly my turn, I finally get picked,
As I prepare to get hit, I am filled with fear and excitement,
As the huge hand powerfully comes at full speed towards me,
He caves my poor soul into the deepest, darkest darkness,
He places me gently on the tall, white tee.
I watch him tentatively as he swiftly swings the hard club up,
Finally, I say, 'I only have a few seconds left to live.'
I feel incredible pain as I land next to the waving red flag,
As quick as a cheetah, I dash for cover in the nearest hole I can find.
Instead of hearing the usual huge groan
From the crowd of people watching,
It turns into an enormous, incredible cheer!
I feel much happier now . . .
Now that I have made someone's dream come true.

Joshua Le Cornu (11)
Victoria College Preparatory School, St Helier, Jersey

Pond

The car trotted towards the fishing pond.
The tyres jogged along, with the engine moaning and groaning,
Not wanting to carry on.
We arrived at the fishing pond, the trees started to whisper
And the creeping, calm, cool breeze of the wind,
Gushed, flushed and rushed onto our skin.
The song of the wind danced
Through the air like a graceful ballerina, leaping.
The beautiful weeds in the pond stared at me,
Wondering what I was doing.
I cast the rod, the line flew in the air,
Darting, carting down, like a torpedo into the water.
The weight dropped down, chatting to the lonely pool,
Trapped, unable to come up.
It screamed to have some air,
But as I cast the line in . . . nothing,
The rod was bare.
But that did not matter,
Because the picnic was calling for me to eat him.
The sun shone on me.
A cool breeze rained on me,
I ate the luxurious sandwiches,
Which were packed like sardines,
Begging to come out.
Now my day was over
And as I walked away to my little stubborn car,
She said, 'Are we going home now?'

Ruben Le Sueur (10)
Victoria College Preparatory School, St Helier, Jersey

Sea

Crashing, bashing against the ragged rocks,
She sits eagerly there, waiting for some helpless prey to gobble up,
Waiting patiently, ready to pounce and cause dreadful chaos,
On a bad, thundery day, you ought to beware,
She won't have any mercy on her pathetic prey,
Slowly, silently, quietly she will jump ferociously on you,
Her relentless mind can go completely berserk,
Whipping her enormous, powerful waves into a giant frenzy,
Knocking helpless boats violently out of their homes,
However, she can also be a calm, peaceful beast,
Her bright blue, azure coat rests gracefully next to the golden sun,
To the small, darting fish she is like an enormous bubble bath,
She laughs and giggles when playful children splash joyfully,
Against her shiny, glistening back,
The shining, hot sun gradually goes down, after a long, busy day,
Then suddenly, out of nowhere, an angry thunderstorm arrives,
Desperately she tries to scramble back where she feels safe;
Next to her good, comforting friend, the golden sand,
But it is no use; she is cut off; separated from her only friends,
She's really depressed and terribly sad now,
Her massive tears fall and break the humongous rocks,
Sad,
Lonely,
Cut off against the world . . .
Until tomorrow.

Max Le Feuvre (10)
Victoria College Preparatory School, St Helier, Jersey

Quad Bike

I am an amazing master of off-roading
I'm a supersonic speed machine
I drift wide at each sharp corner
Gripping the road with all my power and strength
Who am I?
I'm king of legal off-roading
Flying fast through the fresh air
Pushing past all that gets in my way
Pit's here and inviting me to stop
I glug down a soothing cool drink at last
Here I go again, at full speed, screeching
I'm boiling hot and spitting sand out behind me
My brake pads are crying out in pain
As they jam together working hard
Man, I'm totally tired!
I have to keep on racing, determined to finish
Menacing, monstrous machine I am
Master of all mushy mud tracks
Eight hard and challenging laps left
My fast gears changing rapidly
A ferocious roar shouts out behind
An extra springy suspension helps me go
My boiling hot engine slowing down
As I joyously cross the finish line in first place!

Martin Fernando (11)
Victoria College Preparatory School, St Helier, Jersey

Quad Bike

My powerful engine roars loudly into life, like an angry tiger,
I'm off like a speed demon,
I am a master of magnificent mud,
An off-road legend.

I'm drifting, jumping, racing through the sandy dunes,
With my huge suspension, like that of a leaping cat,
I hurl myself eagerly off the sheer ledge
And land heavily into the muddy wastelands . . .

I storm through the wet, wonderful, brown mud,
My engine shouting and screaming to stop,
Other dirty quads, my friends, are stopping helplessly,
Failing to keep up,
I laugh cruelly and spit slimy mud at them with glee!

But in my magnificent moment of glory,
I don't see an evil granite rock waiting up ahead . . .
I hit the lumpy, hard rock with such force, that I flip onto two wheels!
The grand chequered flag is waiting, cheering and waving up ahead.

I try to keep going,
Desperately swerving, dodging, pushing all in my way,
Like a proud lion leaping, I just make it across the black line,
I am overjoyed to have succeeded in my quest to win,
Sweet victory is mine!

Philip Beaugie (11)
Victoria College Preparatory School, St Helier, Jersey

The Plane

The strong, powerful plane sprints up the hot runway
And takes a great leap into the playful air.
The clouds are like mighty, majestic monsters seeking their prey
And the plane becomes scared that home is running away.
Huge, horrible, heavy people walk on his tough tongue
And scream loudly in his delicate ears.
Plane is lost in a world of darkness and monsters
Now he is being pulled strangely along by an invisible hand,
He begins falling, spiralling and plummeting to the unforgiving ground
The growling ground is racing rapidly towards him
He closes his eyes tight and begins to pray.
When he opens his worried eyes, he realises that he is still alive
And more happy people are walking onto him
Some strange men are pointing red lollipops at him.
He races across the dirty runway at top speed again,
He looks and sees that the enormous Earth is sneaking quietly away.
The plane starts to go down gently again to the safe ground again
In the corner of his eye, he notices a blue, glistening runway
He relaxes, drifts and lets himself fall gently asleep.
Suddenly, he splashes into the deep, dark ocean
An almighty explosion roars around,
Will he ever be seen again?

James Bowden (10)
Victoria College Preparatory School, St Helier, Jersey

Poetry Explorers – British Isles

Fear

Fear is as black as the bottomless, fiery pits of the abyss,
It swallows you whole, leaving no scraps!
Everyone despises horrifying fear,
Always Fear comes out at the dead of night,
For his delicious evening meal.
When the happy sun sets,
Worried children hurriedly go into their safe, warm homes.
Fortunately for evil, terrifying Fear,
There is always one unlucky, unsuspecting child who forgets.
Now Fear is on the hunt; in his element.
Fear is like a sneaky, slimy, slithering snake,
Ready to slowly strangle its unwary prey . . .
Fear scuttles down the empty, dark and silent streets,
Creeping past dark houses, causing terrible mischief!
Sneaking past an unlit house, Fear notices all is calm,
Climbing the house, Fear peeps through the dark, dirty windows
And lets out an evil, blood-curdling cry.
Sleeping soundly, a boy is dreaming in his cosy bed,
He wakes up, hearing a rattling on the dark windowpane,
Bravely, he opens the shadowy window and peers outside,
Fear silently climbs up the drain to the roof and scuttles inside,
All that could be heard from outside, is a petrifying scream . . .
Will Fear ever stop being a tormenting, evil thing?

Marcus de la Haye (11)
Victoria College Preparatory School, St Helier, Jersey

Lion On The Prowl

In the grassy plains of Africa, the lion stalks its prey,
Waiting for gazelle or zebra to walk his way.
The lion will pounce on his victim,
Let's hope it's not one of us!
So, beware the stalking lion,
If you happen to see him on the bus!

The lion will jump on a jeep or slide under a fence,
There's no escape from a lion on the prowl -
He might be after us now!

The lion is king of the jungle,
The grassy plains and the zoo.
Watch out, wherever you are,
He might be after you!

In the hot, sticky jungle of Peru,
The lion stalks its prey,
Waiting for chimp or possum to walk his way.

The lion will pounce on its victim -
And let's hope it's not one of us!

So, beware the stalking lion,
If you happen to see him on the bus!

Alec Gibb (8)
Victoria College Preparatory School, St Helier, Jersey

The Basketball

We were crammed in the big, enormous basket,
All waiting to be picked,
Except the smallest, shyest ball - me.
A huge, horrible, heartless hand reached inside the basket,
I was picked up, my stomach lurched!
In addition, I was as scared as a mouse cornered by a cat!
The man bounced me harshly across a wooden corridor,
He came out of a light tunnel, where the massive crowd
Roared like a raging bull.
I cautiously looked around and proudly beamed,
As the crowd cheered.
I was bounced continuously on the court, as hard as rock
The man threw me powerfully at a dangling net,
I flew through the air, like a bird soaring through the sky;
Suddenly, I hit a hard board and bounced into the inviting net.
The crowd screamed and as the team were jumping for joy,
A giant smile spread across my round face.
A piercing, high-pitched whistle screamed,
At the end of the fabulous game,
I was taken back to the boring basket,
The others didn't listen, because they were jealous,
But I didn't care.

Finlay Clayton (10)
Victoria College Preparatory School, St Helier, Jersey

Tornado

I am a raging tornado, which nothing can stop,
Driving the poor villagers to pot,
I hurtle rapidly and rip through an ordinary village,
Which I will certainly pillage,
I can rip off roofs; bring down the strongest houses too,
There is nothing I cannot do!
I spin massive cars round, sucking them effortlessly about
And then spit them disrespectfully out,
In this tremendous fuss, I laugh, *tee-hee!*
Devastated people scream, jump and shout at me,
I rage, ruining and wrecking the beautiful ground,
I can creep up quietly without a sound,
I roar and growl loudly, like a hungry, evil dog
Waiting to be fed, by a dead-cut, screaming log,
'You cannot possibly stop me!' I laugh and cruelly boom,
Then hurtle through the fresh air, with a rapid zoom!
Sadly, I soon die down, leaving an awfully muddy, munched mess,
Sad, distraught people like me less and less,
I am as strong as the strongest god,
Watch and see how I quickly spin; I never plod,
I sleep, tired, nothing is the same,
I then wait two long, dreary years, then strike again!

James Russ (11)

Victoria College Preparatory School, St Helier, Jersey

Fear

My heart is beating fast,
The horror has not yet passed,
I can see it in the corner still,
It's making me feel really ill.

My palms are sweaty, my knees shake,
I wish it would go, for everyone's sake,
It's still there, I see it twitch,
Ouch! All this running has given me a stitch!

I'm frozen to the spot, as it starts to crawl,
Its shadow looms big on the lounge wall,
I can't run and I can't hide,
I feel like my hands and legs are tied.

It's nearer now, I can hardly breathe,
But rooted to the spot, I just can't leave,
Sobbing now, I collapse on the floor
And then I hear the opening of a door.

My mum appears with the Hoover on
And before I know it, the spider's gone,
I can breathe again and move from the spot,
I really must get over the fear that I've got!

Brandon Brawley (10)
Victoria College Preparatory School, St Helier, Jersey

Tidal Wave

I come from deep in the electrifying ocean,
Dragging puny boats down into the deep, dark abyss.
Then I suddenly hit the still, gentle shore,
Chewing unrelentlessly up the calm coastline.
No one can make me hesitate,
I will powerfully destroy all in my mighty path.
I love to lick lovely buildings down to the hard ground
And smack swaying skyscrapers skilfully in their noses.
I am as unstoppable as a burning meteor in its fiery rage,
No one can stop me; I am the all-powerful tidal wave.
I am as menacing as a monster,
I hurdle amazingly over peaceful, sleeping islands,
With an electrifying leap,
Missing them terribly and crushing them under my giant feet.
I love to throw tiny cars about
And punch dull, dreary houses too.
I want to rip the miniature world apart with my icy waters,
Smashing, crashing and bashing everything in my way . . .
In my terribly evil wrath,
Death comes suddenly to all in my death-filled path,
I am the all-powerful tidal wave.

Harry Jones (10)
Victoria College Preparatory School, St Helier, Jersey

The Earth

Powerful Earth was created by an enormous big bang
He started to swirl, twirl and hurl around the flaming hot sun
Earth was as empty as an enormous, dark, black hole
He had no one to play with and felt very sad and lonely
Finally, the most vicious things that ever lived . . . the dinosaurs
Chomped and stomped around on his round body
Ripping large chunks from his green, lush skin
He felt the suffering, as the life-destroying meteor
Came hurtling down from dark, cruel space
Unusual humans came along and built, worked and played
They tried to change him and poked and prodded him
He seemed to like them, but they began to ignore him
They built smelly, filthy cars and all sorts of weird machines
He felt they didn't look after him anymore
A huge, horrid hole started to appear above him
Earth began to feel hot and bothered
Which he did not like and he felt really sad
He wished humans would all stop and leave him alone
He wished he could get rid of these terrible monsters
That treated him so badly
But he didn't count on what would happen next . . .

Cameron Winch (10)
Victoria College Preparatory School, St Helier, Jersey

Four Seasons

In spring, the world leaps like an energetic rabbit,
Small, furry and timid.
His joy blossoms in the glowing sun,
He shakes the gentle wind in the trees,
He springs spring upon winter.
In summer, the world lazes like a Cheshire cat,
Lazy, relaxed and peaceful.
He lies back, purring on the sun-warmed grass,
He rolls over, slowly cooking everything,
He laughs at the funny bird calls.
In autumn, the world retreats, like a frightened squirrel running away,
Frightened by the brown objects swirling down
From the heavens above.
Winter comes as a black demon,
Swirling down from the skies above,
Spiking out across the land,
With a cold heart and a black hide,
The demon pounces, but spring stops him,
The demon . . . is tamed . . .

Guy Pim (10)
Victoria College Preparatory School, St Helier, Jersey

Swan

An elegant beast,
A real beauty in one word;
Wonderfully white.
In a frenzy of feathers,
It has gone and flown away.

Alexander Hodnett (11)
Victoria College Preparatory School, St Helier, Jersey

Poetry Explorers – British Isles

The Venus Fly Trap

The butterfly falls heavily down,
Onto Venus' waiting tongue.

She bites with crooked, gnarling teeth,
As the butterfly lands upon the leaf.

Venus licks her curvy lips,
Smiling as she swings her hips.

That's why no bird or insect,
Should fly too close to her.

The butterfly trudges down her slavering throat,
Into a desert with a watery coat.

Diving into her stomach juice,
Raging like a beast just let loose.

Making the butterfly slightly float,
Venus the fly trap wishes she had an antidote

Against a growling stomach pain,
For the butterfly was a piece of windowpane!

Alexander Howell-Jackson (11)
Victoria College Preparatory School, St Helier, Jersey

The Trenches

There are lice in my pants,
Barbed wire everywhere you look,
The gas is deadly,
Shelling is never-ending,
Machine gunners cut us down.

Charlie Wilding (11)
Victoria College Preparatory School, St Helier, Jersey

Fire

Fire flickered everywhere,
Fire waved her scarlet hair.

Walking on the wooden beams,
Spreading fiery breath, her body gleams.

Splintering, cracking, burning wood,
Fire lifts her scorching hood.

Nothing can extinguish Fire's evil glance,
Destroying everything with a haunting trance.

Singeing ashes flying through the air,
Drifting, settling everywhere.

Nothing now is Fire's friend,
Unwilling to call it the tragic end.

Beckoning everything here, there, everywhere,
Into her burning grasp.

Taking all in with her,
Nothing can ever last.

Alexander Tucker (11)
Victoria College Preparatory School, St Helier, Jersey

Holy Moses

Moses spoke to God
And went and told the Pharaoh,
About frogs and bugs
And death of the first born son,
Moses brought us religion!

Joseph Barette (11)
Victoria College Preparatory School, St Helier, Jersey

The Sea

As I crash down, gorgeous white foam and bubbles,
Pour out from under my beautiful wave,
A noise of crashing, bashing and smashing can be heard,
In all the houses.

I slowly lift the water from my tummy,
Up, up and up and *crash!*
These waves of mine are feisty and furious at night,
Dancing like a hungry wolf.
But at midday, I am as calm as a gleaming blade of grass,
On a midsummer's day.

I am peaceful, calm and a lovely shade of blue,
Suddenly, I begin again - one last *crash!*
My waves smash down . . .
Slowing to a halt, they finish their last, swift movement,
As a tiny bit more of white foam pours out,
Like a tasty smudge of whipped cream,
White as a cloud made of silk,
Still some bubbles left, but only the remains from last night.

Ben Reid (11)
Victoria College Preparatory School, St Helier, Jersey

Football

Cheering and screaming
Kicking of footballs on field
The first goal is scored
The crowd go wilder than dogs
The game won, the crowd go home.

Rory Coughlan (11)
Victoria College Preparatory School, St Helier, Jersey

The Hot Dog

Yum, yum, yum, the hot dog on the plate,
It's like my mum put him there for bait.
I stare at the oven all day long,
Watching as the hot dogs sing their song.
As he comes out of the oven, I can't bear to wait,
To eat this hot dog, it must be my fate.

Slowly I put ketchup on him, as he dances on the plate,
Silently, I have a bite, before it's too late.
While I eat him, like a grizzly bear,
I look at him, as he's really rare.
He starts to slide down my throat,
The bread acts like a wondrous boat.
I eat the rest as well
And that hot dog was really swell!

When I reach for another,
I start to fight with my brother,
I look at the plate,
There is only a crumb - I'm too late . . .

Daniel Ho (11)
Victoria College Preparatory School, St Helier, Jersey

Tornado

As the wicked wind starts to give an outrageous roar,
It forms into a terrifying *tornado!*
It starts to rampage, punching into anything in its way,
Tossing, turning and tipping frightened people over,
The terror sprints rapidly to LA, then on to unaware Vegas,
Grabbing, throwing and kicking,
Even the tremendous King Presley can't stop it,
Twister is as strong as titanium,
The fierce tornado starts to inhale all houses that stand,
Anything the terrible tube doesn't like, is burped and spat out,
As the deadly destroyer creeps silently up
On those who are innocent,
It swallows anything in its destructive path,
It is now in sunny San Francisco,
The turbulent twirler hurls a hideous, horrendous roar,
The monster destroys the glistening Golden Gate,
Suddenly, without warning, it jogs slowly to San Diego,
It is there, it vanishes into a gentle breeze.

Max Rimmer (11)
Victoria College Preparatory School, St Helier, Jersey

Homework

Homework is a pain,
It runs around your brain,
It makes you go insane
And it's pretty lame,
I'd rather play my game.
Homework is a bore,
It makes you want to snore,
It plays with your mind,
It's very hard to find.
The answer to number five,
It's like it is alive
And when it starts to thrive,
It gets hard to survive.
It's like a brain race,
You try to keep a pace,
Then it runs away,
So I say,
I'll leave it for another day!

Ryan Lowe (11)
Victoria College Preparatory School, St Helier, Jersey

Heaven

Some people have their own idea of Heaven,
The one up in the sky.
There are lots of types of Heaven,
But none as good as mine.
He's a sugary snack and delicious to me,
I can't resist when he beckons me.
When I look, he's down on his knees,
I can hear him say sadly, 'Eat me, please!'
When you chew him, he dances on your tongue,
He jazzes up your taste buds and starts to have some fun.
Down your throat, he swiftly slides,
Turning and churning, he gleefully glides,
He has lots of delicious chocolate on his back
And smothered in honey, to make the snack.
I love Heaven, he's so great,
I think he's a real good mate.
Luckily, it's not a crime,
But this lovely Heaven is all mine!

Reuben Gower (10)
Victoria College Preparatory School, St Helier, Jersey

Aston Martin

The race is about to start and Car feels extremely nervous,
The red light flashes and the green light screams at her to go!
She races, booming around the racetrack,
She squeals like an excited little mouse,
Turning, she rips out part of the sharp corner;
Her enormous V8 heart thumping with delight!
Hot, boiling, scorching fire comes out of her curved back
As she roars like a lion, weaving in and out
Of the menacing obstacles that try and catch her.
With her huge, bulging eyes
She watches and hunts down her rival;
The fierce, ferocious Ferrari.
Eventually, having waited patiently,
She sees her moment and flies past, as quick as a dart,
Into first place, where she likes to be.
She stands proud and happy on the podium,
She is as emotional as England when they won the World Cup!
She is looking forward to her next race!

Bradley Rose (11)
Victoria College Preparatory School, St Helier, Jersey

Thunder

Thunder will find you!
He walks unkindly through the dark, menacing sky,
Searching for his long-lost prey.
He roars unanswered commands out to the helpless world,
Far below in his booming voice, terrifying everyone.
Annoying everything in his terrible, destructive path,
He mercilessly destroys it all.
Thunder is an indestructible demon to mankind,
He growls angrily at absolutely everything.
With the help of his friends, endless rain and brilliant lightning,
Thunder annihilates.
All plants and animals perish under his mighty attack,
Thunder terrifies, torments and tortures all form of pointless life,
He is a deep, dark death for your miniscule eardrums,
Bursting them and eagerly burrowing into your puny brain.
Thunder is as terrifying as a huge, black, hairy spider.
Thunder will find you!

James Le Breton (10)
Victoria College Preparatory School, St Helier, Jersey

Cristiano Ronaldo

A tricky trickster
A free kick fantasy
A super shooter
A cool crosser
A tough tackler
A dreadful diver
A Man U masterpiece.

Sam King (11)
Victoria College Preparatory School, St Helier, Jersey

Motorboat

A floating, yellow rocket,
She races keenly at top speed,
Along the deep, dark, blue, smooth water
And dances merrily through the white horse waves.
It is a smooth, speedy, sleek boat,
That has a massive, powerful engine,
That sends her skimming speedily along the calm surface,
She quietly tiptoes along the dark, mysterious sea,
Motorboat powerfully prances along the glistening waters,
Playing happily with her fast friends,
Energetically racing each other joyfully.
She finally gets terribly tired
And staggers, splutters and gasps.
Softly, she moves back to the lonely-looking dock,
She gazes dreamily at the twinkling, smiling night sky
And silently drifts off into a deep sleep,
Waiting patiently for the next change to frolic with her friends.

Max Young (10)
Victoria College Preparatory School, St Helier, Jersey

Window

Here comes the morning breeze, as fast as a sneeze,
All foggy, it's making me steam,
That's what's making me scream!
With the heat on one side
And cold on the other,
I'll need a good clean,
With the sloppy, gloopy, smelly stuff,
That jumps on, not coming off!

I'm feeling all hot, I don't know why,
All there is, is the sunny sky,
I feel like I'm swaying
Through a green field,
But I'm as dirty as mud . . .
I'll need a good clean,
With the sloppy, gloopy, smelly stuff,
That jumps on, not coming off!

Emerson Colback (11)
Victoria College Preparatory School, St Helier, Jersey

The 42-foot Yacht

I skimmed the water, like a surfboard just caught a wave,
Going at five or six knots, cruising slowly,
My engine roaring quietly,
My sails fluttering in the wind like a snake,
Heading for its slow prey,
My wheel turning left and right,
To set myself on course as I speed up.

Round the buoys I go, as fast as a jumbo jet,
Flying at full speed through the air above the clouds.
The water is like a flat piece of paper on a table,
So I can sail smoothly across the ocean, without a bump.
Not a single ripple or wave to be seen.
I smile at a passing boat that sails by,
As slow as me, as slow as you.
Who is that? I thought, thinking long and hard,
Soon, I will be back in the yard.

Reuben Taylor (11)
Victoria College Preparatory School, St Helier, Jersey

Fire

The fire dances round the fireplace
Twisting and turning, as hot as molten lava
If you touch it, you will cry out in pain
The fire clutches your body like a snake.

I am silent, but violent
I burn anything unlucky enough to fall in my swirling flames
Slowly, silently and very carefully
I creep upon you, ready to strike.

When I strike, I crackle an evil laugh
I am gleeful in the burning
I am happy in the heat.

I shake my flames
Cinders grow, flames flicker
All the brightness goes
As I burn out.

Callum Harrison (11)
Victoria College Preparatory School, St Helier, Jersey

Tennis Ball

I quickly woke up, happy, ready to play,
Remembering the time I got stuck in the long, dull hay.
The boy took me out and bounced me hard on the ground,
I was raring to go, just like a hound.
The loud crowd was screaming, roaring and excited,
It was becoming dark, so the floodlights were lighted.
He swiftly threw me high in the air, ready to hit,
He whacked me as hard as a baseball zooming into a mitt.
Suddenly, I was flying swiftly through the cool night air,
I bounced, jumped and spun, as the crowd seemed to stare.
I got whacked again and again and again,
I wished I could hide, safe in my den.
The wicked racket whacked me for the last time,
But the end of the match, I didn't feel fine.
The match was over finally and I was on TV,
I love it when the boy decides to play with me!

Robert Duckett (10)
Victoria College Preparatory School, St Helier, Jersey

The Pig

A muddy smeller
A sty dweller
A swill eater
A four-feeter
A pink porker
A greedy grunter
Pork chops, bacon and sausages,
Mmm . . . delicious!

Max Roantree (10)
Victoria College Preparatory School, St Helier, Jersey

My Friend, Guitar

I looked at Guitar,
He stared back at me,
He yawned.
He stretched his sleek body slowly,
He silently called to me,
His voice sounded like the god of rock himself.
His tan was a brilliant shade of red,
I plucked the string and he started to talk!
About his childhood, when he spoke his first chord
And when Guitar first started to walk!
And his first day of school, when he defeated the bullies,
He gave them broken strings and broken whammies.
And the day when he first got a job,
Teaching music in a music shop,
Heavy metal solos and rock!
Then Guitar said, 'Bye-bye! Come and play me anytime!'

James Jeune (11)
Victoria College Preparatory School, St Helier, Jersey

Cat

A fish eater
A fur licker
A mighty jumper
A bed friend
A terrain adventurer
A milk drinker
A home lover
A dog runner.

Nicholas Darwin (10)
Victoria College Preparatory School, St Helier, Jersey

Elephant Spell

The dragon has breathed his last breath,
You humans will have a painful death.
Smother a poisonous spider,
Cover it in some rare cider.
Bubble, bubble, cauldron hot!
Throw in some vampire bats,
Then chop up a ginger cat,
To make the charm flat.
Stir the beer,
To make it crystal clear.
Bubble, bubble, cauldron hot!
Carefully drop in a free-range chick,
To make the potion snap and click.
Next, throw in a ball and make sure it is kicked,
After that, mix in an elephant's ears
And then wait until the elephant appears.

William Giles (10)
Victoria College Preparatory School, St Helier, Jersey

A Witch

A green monster
A potion maker
A death causer
A complete stranger
A toad turner
A scary danger
A poor tramp
A horrible champ.

Reuben Joseph Falle (11)
Victoria College Preparatory School, St Helier, Jersey

The Beach

Wishy-washy, sand all over my floor,
Being with me is never a bore,
Salty water, squirming around,
Sunbeds and towels laid out on my ground.
Sandcastles and barricades being made,
Lots of games are always played.
People are having a barbeque . . .
How to put up a sunbed - they don't have a clue!
Staring at the water, the lifeguard waiting for a yelp,
Somewhere, far out at sea,
A helpless human is calling for help.
My wailing water, washing him away,
My friend, the sea, is definitely rough today.
The wind whirls frantically up above,
People hate me, people adore me,
But most people, with me, fall in love!

Massimo Furness (10)
Victoria College Preparatory School, St Helier, Jersey

A Grey Wolf

A raging monster
A howling night
A deer supper
A pack leader
An agile chaser
A proud leaper
A claw slasher
A dread victory.

George Donaldson (10)
Victoria College Preparatory School, St Helier, Jersey

The Rampant Sea

As she gallops along the seafront, like a beautiful white horse,
The spiky rocks are set out, like the edge of a green,
Gleaming and spectacular golf course.
While the fish gracefully sleep,
Endangered boats begin to loudly weep.
The boats are now in massive trouble,
When they go down, they will make a humungous bubble.

The beautiful boats whine,
The super sea gallops over and says, 'You're mine!'
She crawls over, like a hungry dog,
She will make BBC a huge Internet blog.
Finally, her long raid is over,
She has destroyed half of the boats in poor old Dover.
She is going to have to pay an expensive fee,
Her name is Rampant Sea.

Elliot Powell (11)
Victoria College Preparatory School, St Helier, Jersey

My Dog, Mona

A loud panter
A food hawker
A fast walker
A light sleeper
A wailing weeper
A mess maker
A bone breaker
A home lover.

Freddie Stein (10)
Victoria College Preparatory School, St Helier, Jersey

A Clock

A corrector of your time,
He hangs on the wall,
Or on your hand,
Waiting for someone to check,
To look or to ask,
So he can correct the seconds
Until important meetings,
Not saying a word
Except the second lasting tick of time,
It's a clock's way of saying,
I'm nearby, waiting.

He's grabbing the numbers
With his hands, keeping them in place
To keep you corrected
Very precise, always precise.

Maximilian Hornby (10)
Victoria College Preparatory School, St Helier, Jersey

Titanic

A heavy hunk
A speedy star
A gigantic gem
A brilliant beast
A fantastic feat
A colossal crash
A little lurch
A woeful wreck.

Ryan Cummins (10)
Victoria College Preparatory School, St Helier, Jersey

The Volcano

He sleeps silently for years on end,
Until the day he angrily wakes,
To wreak havoc on the unsuspecting land,
He grumbles with an empty rumbling belly,
Erupting with unearthly anger and inconsolable rage,
Spitting mountain rock all over everything and anything,
He has no mercy,
His molten lava spreads like liquid plague,
His boiling rage cannot be compared,
He eats and eats without hesitation,
Burning, consuming and digesting his unfortunate victims,
Finally, his lovely, lustful lava is solidifying,
Now he is running, retreating and racing for his home,
Where he sleeps silently once more,
When will he awake to cause havoc and despair . . . ?

Charlie Gicquel (11)
Victoria College Preparatory School, St Helier, Jersey

Tiger

The amazetastic beast stalks its prey
Bounding with fantabulos strides
With its shinetastic fur blowing in the wind
And flyjumping the stream for its breakfast!
Then got very sicked from disease
But the dead prey's blood was everywhere
The amazetastic beast lay
Till both were deaded as each other
Why did the tiger eat the boundjumper's heart?

Garth Jackson (11)
Victoria College Preparatory School, St Helier, Jersey

Wind

The wind is powerful, yet gentle
Like a feather fluttering through the sky,
Only just powerful enough to shift the clouds,
But it's a different story when he invites his friends over ...

When lightning and rain come to play
They thrash around, conjuring storms
Like mean bullies, they crush houses
Uproot trees and wreck pavements
Until they're tired and fall asleep.

Wind is like a baby at night
Terrified, screaming and damaging its cradle
Until it falls asleep . . .
But be aware, when he wakes up
He might be very angry.

Morgan James (10)
Victoria College Preparatory School, St Helier, Jersey

Fire

I dance energetically around the old fireplace
Feeding on the tasty ebony coal.
Coughing and spluttering, I chew up the lush rainforest
Confidently, I stride spookily and silently in your sleeping houses
You will only notice me destroying all, at the last minute.
I'm sinisterly silent, but devastatingly deadly
I destroy all in my destructive path.
I whirl and twirl and spin uncontrollably up dark chimneys
My obliterating life is sadly short
My immense, deadly, fearful heat is incredibly hot
I greedily eat my delicious food, as quick as a speeding car.
Almost as hot as the sun and as sly as a fox
I'm a red-hot flame
I let nothing stand in my way!

Max Jouault (10)
Victoria College Preparatory School, St Helier, Jersey

Julius Caesar

Roman Emperor soon,
Cloak-wearing superman
Giganttourmas house owner
Winning massdistructionating battles
Boldly scoundering forwards
A gang masshated him
They were deathplotting!
Caesar scunderd to court
Got up from his lowthrone
And suffered a heartstabbingly bad death.

Isaac Le Breton (10)
Victoria College Preparatory School, St Helier, Jersey

Bowzer The Dog

Breaknight dawned, the dark fled
And the sun shine slifted through the curtains
Waking the old palloyal pooch, Bowzer
Stretching and yawning, he snouffles his owner
The wet tongue slimifying his face
It is time for the bonehunter to play
Out in the garden, with bouncifying energy
The digduggera sends soil flying
Searching for the hunormas juicy bone he buried yesterday
No bone he found, instead he earthedup
Granny's Sunday nish-gnashers
Grandpa's comfitable gardening boot
And last week's loshlicious leg of lamb
Oh dear, our playpal has problems.

Michael Day (10)
Victoria College Preparatory School, St Helier, Jersey

A Football

He sprints past the keeper,
Small and round.
He's an unstoppable force,
As he whizzes on the ground.
Up into the air and down again,
He's the striker's best friend.
For 90 minutes he works,
Then he takes a big rest.
He waits anxiously,
For his next match.

Ben Timms (10)
Victoria College Preparatory School, St Helier, Jersey

Tree

The tree is like a dead body
Still, quiet and alone
He's waiting for a long time
Waiting forever
He waits and waits and waits
He always waits
Until one day, everyone forgets him
And he rots and rots and rots
And all the leaves fall off
And he rots until he can rot no more
He dies and falls loudly, with a bang
Then the farmer plants another tree
But the same thing happens again
And the next and the next and the next!

Daniel McCarthy (11)
Victoria College Preparatory School, St Helier, Jersey

At Dayfall

At dayfall, the furry little runner comes,
Preening ear, paw and tail.
Hopping through gorse,
Scurrying through fern,
Bobbing playfully on the grassy slopes,
Leaping high and leaping low,
Scattering left and scattering right,
Running to its burrow.
Listening to the sound on the wind,
Ears pricked high and spiked,
Frozen like a statue with fright,
As the predators screech, passing by,
This furry runner never stops,
Through night and day, it hops and hops!

Reid O'Neill (10)
Victoria College Preparatory School, St Helier, Jersey

The Moon

I, the moon, always look down on the spoilt Earth
I see the cushiony clouds slowly plodding around to keep her cool.
I wish I could enjoy the fun and friendly company of people
For I get so terribly lonely with no one to enjoy my qualities.
The only time I am visited, is when people come to explore
They stab my uneven skin with a sharp, spiky, single flag.
They scorch my rough skin on their departure
And leave me alone again.
My forever flaming father, the sun, makes me do the nightshift
I loathe giving the Earth light for long, I'd love to be like her.
I long for attention, like a miniature human needs water to live
And still today I look down with hatred as dark as the underworld
I wait for my revenge!

Nathan de la Haye (10)
Victoria College Preparatory School, St Helier, Jersey

Basketball

He was quickly injected with an enormous syringe,
The basketball player pumped it into his round, plump body,
He then began to come alive and grow.
All the time, he was waiting, worrying and whimpering,
He lay on one edge of the sideline wall,
Separating him from the fun of the game.
Some huge hands came and picked him up with excitement,
The tall basketball player bounced, passed
Then threw him away at great speed,
He orbited into the air, like a flaming rocket,
The jumping player scored . . . no, ball scored!
The excited player cheered with him for joy,
They both played together for evermore!

Solomon Warner (11)
Victoria College Preparatory School, St Helier, Jersey

Animals

Some are big
And some are small
There's pictures of some
On the gallery wall
Some are thin
And some are fat
Some like to lie on your doormat
Some have tails
Some do not
Some like to live in places hot
I like pigs, the same with bats
But all I'm allowed is
A boring cat!

Jacob Hill (9)
Victoria College Preparatory School, St Helier, Jersey

Fire

Fire treads through trees
It kills everything, from redwoods to weeds
Fire kills every living thing
The flame loves to sing.

The flame laughs and cackles
With deafening sparks and crackles
The fire zooms off in a blast
All that's left are broken trees and dead grass.

What can stop this awful slaughter?
Nothing much, just a bit of water
That's all that can stop a murderous bushfire
Believe me, it's all we have, our state is dire!

Evan Spencer (10)
Victoria College Preparatory School, St Helier, Jersey

Star

I shoot swiftly through the air, like a cheetah catching his prey,
As I sparkle through the twilight zone hoping to play.
Glistening brightly whilst I watch the dull Earth in the night sky,
Thinking, *will I ever have a friend and why?*
I spin, sparkle and glisten, while I'm being watched from below,
But no one wants to watch me and my magical, sparkly glow.
The other planets are so stupid not wanting to play,
Jupiter told the dangerous, dark black hole to go spin away!
I'm a sparkling, silver servant of the Sun, Earth and Moon,
But when they're on holiday, I'm left in a deep, dark gloom.
They're back now and I won't be in a terrible fright,
I'm all ready for a good, brilliant, bright night!

Jamie Smith (10)
Victoria College Preparatory School, St Helier, Jersey

At Dayfall

At dayfall, the hip-hopper comes,
Hipping along the splitty-splatty lily pads,
He dips and dives down and down
And then, with a jipperty joy, he jumps back up.
At midday, the hip-hopper comes,
He hops along the splitty-splatty lily pads,
Fly-a-catching and bug-o-chomping as he goes.
At dawn, the hip-hopper comes,
He hops along the splitty-splatty lily pads,
With slippery flap and a slopperty slip
He basks his flippy, flappy flubber
In the warm, fizzy, fuzzy midday sun.

Max Shepherd (10)
Victoria College Preparatory School, St Helier, Jersey

Wind

He dazily glides, soaring through the sky,
Dreaming gratefully, singing out like he doesn't care.
He loves to play with children and their kites,
Pulling and pushing them all over the place
Having so much fun, being a good boy for once!

But when he's angry, it's quite a different story
Instead, he rampages through the park
Tearing trees, limb from limb, scattering them all over the place
Digging up dirt and slamming against the floor
And he screams and screams, the endless screaming
When will it end?

Dylan Kempster-Smyth (10)
Victoria College Preparatory School, St Helier, Jersey

Young Writers Information

We hope you have enjoyed reading this book - and that you will continue to enjoy it in the coming years.

If you like reading and writing poetry drop us a line, or give us a call, and we'll send you a free information pack.

Alternatively if you would like to order further copies of this book or any of our other titles, then please give us a call or log onto our website at www.youngwriters.co.uk

Young Writers Information
Remus House
Coltsfoot Drive
Peterborough
PE2 9JX
(01733) 890066